MW00935109

FINAL LIFE

BOOK 1 IN THE FINAL LIFE SERIES

ROSE GARCIA

For Augie.

CHAPTER *One*

THUMPING MUSIC AND HOWLS OF laughter echoed from the end of the dark cul-de-sac as I walked to the home of Infiniti Clausman—a girl I hadn't met yet. She found me online after coming across my posts about moving to Rolling Lakes, most of which contained the words "sucked," "stupid," and "dumb." Several messages later, we found out we lived on the same street and that I'd be going to her school. And now, I was heading to her party.

With each step I twisted my hair tight around my finger, my heart beating out of control because I sucked at meeting new people. And then a bug bit me, right on my arm. I smacked it, slowing down my pace so I could examine my hand under the streetlight. Peering at the flattened form, I finally recognized it as a mosquito. Its crushed body oozed with blood. I wiped it away on my jeans, disgusted at all the germs on my skin, when something else occurred to me. How could there be mosquitoes the day after Thanksgiving?

So far, I hated everything about hot and humid Houston, Texas.

Passing the homes, and almost to my destination, I thought the structures all looked the same—two-story, red-brick, cold and lifeless. There weren't any porches like back home in Elk Rapids, Michigan. No charm. Worse than that, the tiny backyards were all fenced in, like personal prison yards. Would I ever get used to this?

Coming up to Infiniti's, I watched as bodies poured in and out of the house. Beer cans and plastic cups were scattered about the yard. Even though Infiniti seemed nice enough, fear of walking into a party alone and not knowing a single soul settled in. I turned to go back home when I heard my name from a group of people standing around the front door.

"Hey! Are you Dominique Wells?"

Crap, now I was stuck. I drew in a deep breath before turning back around to see a petite figure coming my way. "Yeah. Are you Infiniti?"

"The one and only!" She had long, wavy black hair and wore tight cut-off shorts with cowboy boots and a black shirt with a purple peace sign. She took me by the arm, as if we had known each other for years. Her eyes were big and brown, her smile wide, and her tiny frame barely reached my shoulders. "Come on, you've got tons of people to meet!"

The first person I met was Veronica, Infiniti's best friend. Tall like me, she had long bleached blond hair that cascaded down her back. Dark foundation and heavy, pink blush made her face way too dark for her light-skinned neck. She fluttered her tarantula-like eyelashes disapprovingly at me while she scanned every detail of my outfit. Luckily, I didn't have to stand there too long as Infiniti ushered me through the crowded house and to the kitchen. By the time we got there, I had met around a dozen people and everyone seemed pretty cool.

Maybe moving here wouldn't be so bad after all.

Infiniti grabbed a beer, opened it, and shoved it in my hand. "I know it sucks being new because I've so been there. But if you stick with me, I'll help you out." Before I could say anything, someone from across the room shouted her name. "I'm coming!" she called out. She brought her attention back to me. "I'll be right back. Okay?"

"Sure. Don't worry about me." I downed the beer in four gulps, hoping it'd help me relax, but it didn't. Standing there by myself, I felt more out of place than ever. The music grew louder, and everyone started dancing. Back home I would've been in the middle of the crowd, having a great time, but now I was the outsider. And I hated it. I tossed the can in the trash and made my way to the front door.

"Dominique! Where ya going?" It was Infiniti, rushing up to catch me before I walked out of the house. The pungent, woodsy stench of weed hung thick on her clothes. "You just got here!"

The last thing I wanted to do was stay, but I also didn't want to be rude to my first new friend. "Well, I'm pretty tired from all the unpacking, but I guess I can stay a little longer."

Infiniti smiled. "Good! Come on. Let's go upstairs to my room for a quick sec. I wanna show you something."

She trotted upstairs and I followed. I half-expected to see her mom come out of one of the bedrooms, but didn't. "So… is your mom around?"

"Infiniti's mom is never around." I turned to see Veronica behind me and gulped. There was something about her I didn't like, and it wasn't just her caked-on makeup.

"Yeah," Infiniti chimed in. "She works a lot, and she's a single mom, so most of the time I'm solo." She stopped at a black door with a giant purple "*I*" painted on it. "You guys, ready for some fortune-telling?"

What? Every scary movie involving the paranormal swirled in my mind—movies I had never liked watching even though my friends loved them. My stomach clenched, my spine tingled, and something inside me said not to do it.

"You know, it's late," I said with a nervous laugh. "And I'm exhausted. I should really go."

Infiniti's mouth fell open. She placed her hand on her hip and stuck her right foot out. "You can't leave now! Not before the fun part! Besides, now that we're neighbors and all, we should get to know each other. Consider me your…" I waited for her to finish, but she seemed to be searching for the right word. "I got it! senior advisor! That's it! I'm your senior advisor!"

Infiniti let out a series of giggles. The tension inside me eased up, until I glanced at stone-faced Veronica.

"Chill out! Please!" Infiniti said to her.

Veronica flashed a fake smile and started

playing with a strand of hair. "I'm chill. Now can we hurry this up? Trent should be here any minute now and I don't want to miss him."

"Trent?" I asked.

"Trent Avila," Infiniti explained. "Veronica's ex. They broke up two months ago, and she's trying to get him back."

Veronica glared at Infiniti. "Seriously? You gonna tell everyone?"

Infiniti rolled her eyes. "I'm sorry, but everyone knows!"

Veronica crossed her arms and huffed. "Are we gonna do this, or what?"

Their friendship reminded me of a soap opera, and I was beginning to wish I hadn't come over after all.

"Yes, we're gonna do this," Infiniti said, turning the knob and opening the door. We stepped into the lit room. Infiniti turned off the light and shut the door. Darkness enveloped us. I squinted, hoping to find a sliver of light to focus on, but couldn't find one.

"We need to hold hands and stand in a circle," Infiniti instructed. "I need to announce our presence before we open the cards."

Cool fingers touched my arm, and I jumped. "Dominique, it's me," Infiniti laughed.

"Sorry," I said. Her small hand made its way to mine, and she took it with a firm grip.

I extended my other hand and searched the shadows for Veronica when her long and slender hand met mine.

"Are we all holding hands now?" Infiniti asked.

"Yeah," Veronica answered. "Now let's get on with it."

Infiniti began whispering words I couldn't make out. I tried to pay attention, but my thoughts kept straying to my messed-up life. I had moved thousands of miles to a new city during senior year, and now stood in the middle of a pitch-black room with two girls I didn't even know. Worse yet, we were about to play some sort of psychic card game. The loud, thumping music from downstairs vibrated the walls, almost in unison with my pounding heart. As much as I wanted to leave, I didn't.

"Okay," Infiniti said when she finished. "We're ready now!"

She released my hand and strode past me, the odor of weed following her every move like a needy companion. She fumbled around for a few seconds, tripping over things and bumping into the wall, when the crank of a switch sounded. The dark room illuminated with a hazy glow. I had to blink a few times before noticing a sheer purple scarf covering a lampshade. In fact, her entire room oozed purple from top to bottom. The only break in the color scheme was her black comforter.

I kept studying Infiniti's messy and cluttered room when my gaze met Veronica's. Her brown, shallow eyes studied me for a moment before she sat on Infiniti's bed. I wanted to ask her what her problem was, but stopped myself. The last thing I needed was an enemy at a new school.

With my attention back on Infiniti, I noticed a brown stick of incense in her hand. She tilted it and lit the end with a lighter, fanning it until the blue flame went out and all that was left was the burning end. She stuck it in a small cone on her desk and then opened the drawer. She brought out a black wooden box and sat next to Veronica. She scooted over and made room for me.

Her personality switched from playful to serious. "These are the new Oracle cards Jan gave me the other day." She opened the box, brought out a sheet of paper, and starting reading. "These cards are designed to help you manifest your goals, life purpose, and divinely inspired dreams. Proper use will help you swim into the ocean of your unconscious mind, where profound thoughts and feelings can create — or block — your heart's desire."

She rubbed her hands all over the box with an excited grin. As she did, I could've sworn the room darkened. Infiniti and Veronica didn't react, and I wondered if my eyes were playing tricks on me.

"Who's Jan?" I asked.

"Jan's the cool, old lady who lives across the street from me," Infiniti said. "I'll have to introduce you guys. She's totally into all this stuff, and she's very" — she held up her hands and made quotation marks with her fingers — "spiritually connected."

Infiniti shuffled the cards. The woodsy aroma from the incense, which had started out faint, grew stronger by the second. My head started to spin. My stomach tumbled. I grabbed my knees, hoping Infiniti and Veronica wouldn't notice my reaction to the stench, and did my best to steady myself.

Infiniti handed the deck to Veronica. "Think of a question."

Veronica held the cards with both hands. She closed her eyes for a moment before handing them back. Infiniti fanned them out on the bed. "Now pick one," she instructed Veronica.

Infiniti leaned toward me as Veronica scanned the cards. "The card's message will answer her question," Infiniti whispered. "And the question must never be revealed."

Veronica picked her card and showed it to us. On one side was a picture of a mermaid brushing her long hair. On the other side was the message.

"Self-Forgiveness," Veronica read. "Let go of old guilt and release your past mistakes. Remember to guard yourself from evil thoughts."

Infiniti's mouth fell open. "Holy shit," she said. "It's Trent. You need to let go of him and your guilt for cheating on him. You know, move on."

Veronica cast her eyes down, and I thought I saw them water. I fidgeted, feeling more uncomfortable than ever. Maybe Veronica wasn't so bad after all.

Infiniti rested her hand on Veronica's leg. "You okay?"

"I'm fine." Veronica's back stiffened before she continued. "Come on, let's do you now."

"Whatever you say," Infiniti muttered. She took the cards, closed her eyes and handed the deck to Veronica. Following Infiniti's lead, Veronica fanned the cards out on the bed. Infiniti opened her eyes and picked one. It had a picture of a forest with young mermaids having a tea party on a stone in a river. "Friendship," she read. "Make a date for a play day with one or more friends. Release yourself in laughter and love."

She sighed, looking disappointed with her selection, but then cheered up. "Let's hang tomorrow!"

We laughed — except Veronica who had taken out her phone and was texting someone.

Infiniti ignored her while she gathered up the cards, shuffled them, and handed them to me. "You're next, Dominique."

Thick incense coated my throat as I reached for the cards. When I touched the deck, a jolt of electricity shot through me as if I had made contact with a stun gun. I pulled my hand back and winced hard. When I opened my eyes, I saw a red landscape — empty and quiet. Where was Infiniti's purple room? The booming music? The odor of incense and weed? Where... was... I?

I spun around, seeing nothing but red sky and red sand, when a flicker of familiarity registered with me. I knew this place, but how? My gaze settled on the crimson dirt at my feet when a dull, throbbing ache crept up my neck, hovering right at my hairline. I reached out to touch the spot when a stinging clap hit my face. I blinked, then saw Infiniti's tiny frame in front of me, her hand raised. She had slapped me, and was about to slap me again when she stopped short.

"Dominique? Are you like tripping or something?"

"No! I ... uh..." My heart slammed against my chest. My throat had completely dried over.

9

The hazy purple room seemed to close in on me.

"She's totally high," Veronica said, her arms crossed and her head cocked to the side. I had no idea what I'd done to piss her off, but she definitely didn't care for me. And I *really* didn't care for her.

I brought my hand to my cheek, at the spot that now burned. "You know, I'm not..." I stammered for a moment, trying to figure out what to say, my thoughts taking me back to that red vision. "Feeling well. I better go."

"No! You can't!" Infiniti jumped in front of the door, arms spread wide. "The cards are in play. If we don't finish, it'll bring bad luck on all of us. We don't need bad luck."

Everything inside me said to run, but at the same time, I wanted to see if I would go back to that red place. Infiniti sensed my hesitation, made a move for the cards, and extended them out to me. "Here, ask your question."

The room grew smaller, the darkness thicker. With a slow reach, I touched the deck. A shock connected at my fingers and then faded away.

"Whoa," Infiniti said. "I saw that! I saw a white spark at your fingertips!"

Veronica leaned forward, suddenly interested in me. "What? A spark?"

"Yeah, Dominique shocked the cards when she touched them."

My hands wrapped around the cards. I waited to see the red desert again, but nothing happened.

"That was way cool," Infiniti said. "You must have good energy."

Good energy? I didn't think there was anything good about what I had seen, or about the pain at the back of my neck. In fact, the whole night sucked. And then I wondered if she had seen the spark the first time I touched the cards.

"Did you see anything when you first handed me the cards?"

"No." Infiniti inched closer to me, her eyes growing wide again. "Did you?"

"No. I, uh, didn't."

"Come on," Veronica whined. "This is taking way too long, and I want to get back to the party."

"Fine," Infiniti said to her. "Dominique, think of your question."

I closed my eyes and concentrated on my question. I thought of how miserable I was with my move, how pissed I was at my parents, then my thoughts turned to the red desert I had just seen. There were way too many things crammed in my head, so I thought to myself, *tell me what I need to know.*

When I handed the deck back to Infiniti, she fanned the cards out on the bed. I drew one and studied it for a moment. It had a picture of a young mermaid pushing a dolphin down into the water, helping it reach the other dolphins below the surface. I cleared my throat. "You're Being Helped. There are heavenly forces working behind the scenes to help you, even if you don't see results yet."

CHAPTER *Two*

MY THOUGHTS FLOODED WITH MY vision. The throbbing at the back of my neck lingered. My hand eased up to the spot when I thought of the birthmark I had there. I gave it a rub, wondering if I should tell Infiniti and Veronica what I had seen, but quickly decided against it. They probably wouldn't believe me, especially since I hardly believed it myself.

Veronica pulled the scarf off the lamp and stood in front of the vanity mirror. She opened a drawer, took out a bag of makeup, and began putting on even more black eyeliner. With light skin and blond hair, the eyeliner really stood out, but not in a good way.

Infiniti walked to the door, and I followed. This was my chance to get out of there. As I made my way past Veronica, I caught a glimpse of myself in the mirror. Damn. My face looked deathly white, like I had seen a ghost.

"You want some makeup, too?" Infiniti asked.

I couldn't help but think she was telling me

I needed some, especially since I knew I did. "That's all right. I need to go anyway."

"Okay. I'll go downstairs with you, then." She stopped at the door and eyed Veronica. "You coming?"

"In a minute. Y'all go on." Finished with the eyeliner, she moved on to blood-red lipstick. "Gotta make sure I look perfect."

Infiniti studied Veronica for a moment. "Ya know, you should forget about Trent and move on. The spirits never lie."

Veronica blotted her lips on a tissue. "I didn't ask for your opinion."

"Okay," Infiniti said, holding up her hands as if in surrender before letting out an exasperated sigh.

Back downstairs, the number of people had more than doubled. I could easily slip away without anyone noticing me, as if anyone had even noticed me in the first place.

"Thanks for having me over, Infiniti."

"Any time. And I was serious about knowing what it's like to be new. I moved here from Pennsylvania two years ago, so I know the drill. We can even hang tomorrow if you want."

"Maybe," I said, hoping it wouldn't include Veronica. "Text me."

Turning toward the door, and steps away from being outside, someone took my arm and pulled me to a halt. Thinking it was Infiniti stopping me for another psychic session, I turned to face her with an "I don't think so" face, but instead found myself in front of a super hot guy. He had tan skin with the bluest of eyes, a light blue you see at the edge of the bay back home. His hair was a sun-kissed brown with bangs that hung slightly on the long side. He was taller than me, but not by much, and from the way his shirt hugged his body, he was nicely sculpted.

"You're not leaving, are you?" he asked with a casual smile. "I just got here."

"Oh, well, uh. Yeah, I am."

Infiniti had left me, but returned with a curious look on her face. "Do y'all know each other?"

He stuck out his hand for a shake. "Not yet," he said. I hesitated a moment, unsure if I should take it. He leaned in. "Come on, I won't bite."

With a smile, I placed my hand in his. His skin felt nice and warm, and my cheeks filled with heat. "I'm Dominique Wells, and I was just leaving."

"I'm Trent Avila, and I was just entering."

Shit! It was Veronica's ex. He stepped closer to me and a hint of clean, fresh soap drifted my way. "You sure you can't stay?"

"No!" Veronica called from the stairs, her eyes shooting daggers at me. "I mean, no, she can't. She's tired. Isn't that right, Dominique?"

I glanced at Infiniti, hoping she'd rescue me from Veronica's nasty glares, but she didn't seem to notice them.

"She's right. I need to. I'll see you guys later." I gave a wave, then made a quick exit.

The moist and sticky Texas air clung to my body as I hurried home, my heart beating so loud I could hear it pulsing in my ears. As if Veronica's ex taking interest in me wasn't bad enough, what the hell had I seen when I touched those cards? I had to get myself under control before I got home. If I didn't, Mom would ask a ton of questions — and the last thing I needed was for her to find out about the beer, the weed, and the card game. She'd freak.

I grabbed my hair and began twisting it in a knot, the red vision clear in my mind. *I'm okay*, I said to myself over and over. *It was nothing*. After taking several long and deep breaths, my nerves settled and my heart slowed to a somewhat normal pace. I took my phone out of my pocket and texted a few friends back home, but no one responded. Everyone had already moved on without me.

I had never felt so alone in my life.

When I got home, Mom and Dad were in the dining room. They hovered over maps and ancient documents that covered the table, no doubt researching their latest geological project and the reason we had moved to Houston.

Without stopping, I hollered that I was going to bed and made my way for the stairs, but Mom had other ideas. "Dominique, come back for a minute. We want to hear about the party."

I paused, my eyes darting to the safety of the second floor before giving a silent exhale and joining them. Why couldn't they leave me alone?

I entered the dining room. "It was good."

"Good? That's it?" Mom asked.

"Yeah, you know —" My mind flashed to my red vision. "A regular party."

Dad lowered the papers in his hands and stared at me. "Are you sure?"

A nervous twinge struck the pit of my stom-

15

ach. Could he smell the weed? I backed up a little, pretending to scratch my leg. "Yes, I'm sure. What about you guys? How's your research going?"

Dad looked at Mom, then back at me. "It's coming along." His bloodshot eyes said otherwise. For as long as I could remember, they were always filled with worry. I knew the move here was as hard on him as it was on me. And even though I wanted to make him feel better, wanted to somehow reach out to him, I didn't. I still couldn't forgive him for ruining my life. Not yet anyway.

I gave a fake yawn. "I'm going to bed."

"Good night," Mom said.

My mind kept flashing to my vision as I went upstairs, got ready for bed, slipped on my ear buds, and huddled under my covers. The rhythmic drumming and synthesizer-laced music started to calm me. *Relax*, I kept telling myself. *It was nothing.* After a while, my out of control thoughts calmed down. My tense muscles loosened. I took out my ear buds and placed them on my nightstand. My heavy eyelids started to close when a flashing bright light filled my room. I covered my face, irritated that someone had turned on my light.

"Not cool," I said, uncovering my eyes. Instead of seeing mom or dad, I found myself in the red desert again. Scorching heat blasted my lungs and burned my eyes and nose. My gaze drifted upward. Flashes of light illuminated the red sky. Panic overtook me, followed by the feeling that I had been here before, that I knew this place, that I dreaded this place.

My hands instinctively went to the back of my neck, knowing the pain would come again, and it did. But this time it wasn't a subtle creeping sensation, but more of a shooting, searing pain. I spun around, searching for the source, but again I was alone. Without even thinking, my mind called out for help, my voice so loud in my head it echoed all around me.

"Dominique!" a voice hollered.

The red desert vanished. Dad leaned over me, his strong hands grasping my shoulders. It took me a while to recognize the safety of my room.

"Dominique," he said again. "Are you okay?"

"Dad?" I searched the room, looking for the red landscape. "What happened?"

He sat on the edge of the bed. Mom stood behind him. "You were dreaming," he said. "But your eyes were open."

"Open?" I asked.

Mom touched my forehead. "Yes, wide open, like you were awake."

The dull, aching throb remained at the back of my neck, the only evidence that my vision was real. I wanted to touch it, but not in front of them. For some reason I didn't want them to know what I had seen.

"Dominique," Mom pressed. "What is it?"

Flashes of red filled my eyes, and my heart started racing again. "I guess the exhaustion from the move is getting to me."

I bit the inside of my cheek. *Go*, I thought over and over in my head. *Please*. My throat tightened as I forced my tears to stay buried deep down inside me. Finally they left, and I was alone, the dread and despair from the red desert my only companion. Then I thought of the card I had drawn at Infiniti's. *There are heavenly forces working behind the scenes to help you, even if you don't see results yet.* I had never believed in God, or heaven, but I hoped somebody out there was helping me, because I really needed it.

CHAPTER Three

Moving across the country during senior year had one huge benefit. My parents had said they'd buy me a new car. Unfortunately, they were so busy with the house and the new job they had to put it off for a few weeks. Saving myself from having to take the school bus, or worse, having to get a ride from my parents, I decided to ask Infiniti if she could help me out until we could go car shopping. She showed up at my door before I could text her.

"Hey," she said with a smile that displayed her perfectly straight and tiny teeth. Bubbly and full of life, she radiated positivity. "I thought I'd come check on you before school starts tomorrow. I also wanted to apologize about Veronica. She can be a total bitch sometimes, but she's actually pretty cool. I promise."

I blew out a breath of relief. "I'm so glad you said something because I swear she hates me." My thoughts went to Trent, Veronica's ex who had come up to me right before I left.

"Nah," Infiniti said. "She's insecure, that's all. You'll like her once you get to know her."

I wasn't so sure about that.

"I'm heading home from a quick walk and thought I'd stop and see if you wanted to come over. My mom's not home."

I didn't need to think twice about getting out of my new house. Plus, I had already decided to forget about my visions, Veronica, and Trent so I could concentrate on adjusting to my new life. Maybe if I did, everything would be better and I would feel normal again like I had back home. Hanging out with Infiniti might be the perfect thing for me.

"Going down the street!" I called out, shutting the door behind me before my parents could respond.

"So," she said. "You're super pissed at your parents?"

Feeling bad for being so angry, but knowing she'd understand because she had been through something similar, I asked, "Is it that obvious?"

She laughed. "Kinda."

Feeling comfortable around her, I went on. "They said they'd buy me a car when we got here, but who knows when they'll actually get around to it."

"You can ride with me," she offered. "Problem solved."

"That would be so awesome, and I was actually going to ask you, but are you sure?"

"Of course! What are friends for?" She stopped in front of her house, but eyed the house across the street. "Oh, hey, I've got an idea. Let's go to

Jan's."

"Jan?" A shiver ran down my back. She had used that name when we played the cards.

"Yep, Jan. She's the lady who gave me the cards we played with. I want you to meet her. Come on."

My pulse raced as images of the red desert danced before my eyes. "Infiniti," I said, following her across the street. "I'm not so sure—"

"Jan's awesome. If anything, she always gives me great advice on things. You know, like a trusted grandma or something."

Curiosity made me follow her, even though a hint of fear had settled in my gut. Jan lived in a two-story traditional home with off-white stone and brick. She had interesting and unusual art displayed in her front yard: a copper pole with a blue ball on top, a tree decorated with hanging forks and spoons, and pieces of colorful tile bordering her shrubs. When we approached the house, the front door opened almost magically, as if Jan knew we were coming.

Jan looked completely different than what I had pictured. She stood about six feet tall, with puffy, shoulder- length blond hair. Deeply etched wrinkles lined her lips and blue-green eyes. I figured she was in her early sixties. Although sunny and warm outside, at least in the mid- eighties, she wore a long, black-sleeved turtleneck; a multi-colored, ankle-length plaid skirt; and white athletic socks with black loafers.

"Hi, Jan," Infiniti said. "This is our new neighbor down the street, Dominique."

Jan stood at the doorway. She studied me

with a penetrating gaze. I wanted to look away, but couldn't. Her stare held me captive. "You don't sleep well, dear. Do you?"

My skin lined with goose bumps. How could she know that? "No, I don't."

"Since when?" she asked.

Her voice commanded me to answer, even though I didn't want to. "Since moving here last week."

"Whoa, Jan, how did you know that?" Infiniti asked.

Jan's eyes remained on my face while heat crept up my cheeks.

"Jan," Infiniti said with a little force behind her voice, breaking the awkward silence. "Are you okay?"

"Yes—Yes. I, well, never mind. Come in, Infiniti, and welcome, Dominique. Welcome to Houston and to the fine subdivision of Rolling Lakes. I'm Jan Kelly. But please, call me Jan." Her deep voice almost vibrated within me. She held out her hand and gave me a firm handshake. Her skin was thick, wrinkly, and warm.

"Thank you, Jan. It's nice to meet you."

Her house sparkled with cleanliness. Her walls were a crisp white. Shiny, dark wood lined the floors. Like an art gallery, paintings covered her walls from floor to ceiling. Most were of woodsy landscapes and floral arrangements, except for one. It was a little girl with long, white hair and big, green eyes. For a minute there, I thought her eyes were following me, and I found myself avoiding the portrait. The furnishings were dark antiques, accented with crystal vases and bowls. But what struck me the most was the overpowering smell of vanilla that hung in the air.

"Your home is very nice," I said.

"Thank you, my dear. I enjoy having beautiful things around me."

Jan led me and Infiniti to a blue couch. Its wood trim curved down a little in the middle, reminding me of a couch you might see in an old-fashioned movie. She motioned for us to sit while she made herself comfortable on a black-and-white striped chair. She grabbed a pen and paper from an oversized, dark wooden chest that served as her coffee table.

"I'm going to tell you your soul lives," Jan said.

I glanced at Infiniti from the corner of my eye, wondering if she was as freaked out as me, but I couldn't tell. "Soul lives?" I asked, trying to disguise the fear in my voice.

"Numerology tells us that we have nine soul lives on this Earth. Nine tries to get it right, or nine tries to do what needs to be done before we pass on to the other side."

I sat there, interested and scared all at the same time, wondering which soul life I was living, curious if I needed to do something specific to pass on, recalling the feeling of dread in that red desert which reminded me of death.

"Let's start with you, Dominique. What year were you born?"

"1995."

"The month?"

"January."

"And the day?"

"The second."

"Ah, a little over a month away," Jan whispered. She wrote the numbers down: 1995, 1, 2, one on top of the other, and added them. The total was 1998. She crossed out the nines until there was only the one and the eight. She added them to get nine. She circled it. Her gaze pierced right through me, her brow furrowed, the lines on her face looked pronounced and worry-filled. "This is your last life." The vanilla smell in the house grew stronger. "You better get it right this time."

My thoughts flooded with my vision. Jan leaned forward as if trying to read my mind. I did my best to shut off my thoughts, just in case. Thankfully, her attention left me when the booming chime of a clock from somewhere in the house erased the silence.

She turned her attention to Infiniti. "Now you, my dear."

Infiniti, eager to go next, blurted out, "1995, March the first."

Jan wrote the numbers: 1995, 3, 1, and added them. The total was 1999. She crossed out the nines, leaving the one. "Ah, you're a one. You're brand new."

While Infiniti chatted about senior year, Jan's eyes kept searching mine, her gaze smothering me until I almost couldn't breathe. I had to get out of there.

"Thank you for having me, Jan. But I better get home. I've got tons to do before school tomorrow."

I made my way to the door and Infiniti followed.

"Certainly," Jan replied, her head cocked to the side, her eyes still glued on me.

Once outside, I gulped in the fresh air, erasing the vanilla scent from my lungs and replacing it with the smell of dirt and trees.

Infiniti stretched her arms. "I'm starving, and I've got a pantry full of snacks. Or do you really need to go home?"

"Food sounds good," I muttered, my mind replaying the penetrating, eerie and all-knowing look on Jan's face while she had studied me.

We went to Infiniti's and headed straight for the kitchen.

"How does it feel to be on your last life?" she asked me while she rifled through her snack options.

"You don't believe in that stuff, do you?" Shivers rippled through me, and I wondered if I was trying to convince her, or me.

Infiniti shrugged her shoulders. "Why not? It's fun."

Sitting on a stool by the kitchen counter I said, "I don't know. It seems so freaky."

Infiniti wiggled her fingers. "Totally freaky," she said with a giggle. "And speaking of freaky, Trent asked a lot of questions about you last night."

"He did? Oh, no."

"Yep, and Veronica was pissed. I totally had to calm her down." She popped a Twinkie in her mouth and handed one to me.

"Great," I said, not wanting to be the hated new girl before starting school. My stomach tightened and I pushed the Twinkie away.

"Don't worry about her. She's always pissed about something. Besides, she had her eye on someone else by the end of the night anyway. So you're cool."

"Good. The last thing I need is to get caught up in drama." I thought of the red vision, the card I had drawn, and now the thing about my soul life. "Besides, I plan to keep my head down, finish this year, and head back North for college."

Infiniti had downed her Twinkie and shoved another in her mouth. "You know, I like you, Dominique. You've got it all figured out. I think we're gonna be good friends, you and me."

She was so tiny, her arms and legs like twigs, and I couldn't help but wonder where she put all the calories. She was also really friendly, and I liked that about her. I smiled. "Yeah, that would be great."

As I let myself out, I noticed an Ouija board on the bookshelf. I hadn't seen one of those in years. Somehow, I wasn't surprised at all to see it there.

THE HOUSE WAS EMPTY WHEN I got home. I grabbed a bottle of water from the fridge, went upstairs, and flopped on my bed. My thoughts filled with my encounter with Jan. The way she had stared at me was not normal. Wanting to take my mind off her, I focused on my room. The soft blues calmed me, and suddenly, I felt like I was back home at Elk Rapids Beach where you could walk out for what seemed like forever and the crystal-clear, calm water would never go past your shoulders. The slamming of the downstairs kitchen door interrupted my thoughts.

"Dominique? Honey? Can you come down here?" It was Mom.

When I entered the kitchen, I was shocked to see a guy with Mom and Dad. He was well over six feet tall, lean, with messy blond hair. He had angular features and looked like he had stepped out of a high fashion magazine. He tilted his head and narrowed his eyes as if he recognized me. But I knew there was no way. I would've remembered someone like him.

"Dominique, this is Farrell Walker," Dad said. "His parents work with us. He's going to stay here while they're out of town on business."

"He's also a senior, and he'll be new at the school too, so you won't be alone," Mom added, looking a little nervous.

Farrell came up to me and extended his hand like Trent had. Except where Trent had been flirty and friendly, Farrell was serious and formal. "I'm Farrell Walker. It's nice to meet you, Dominique."

When I placed my hand in his, a tingle struck my fingers. My body tensed. I thought for sure I'd see the red desert again, but didn't. Instead, a warm and peaceful feeling spread throughout my body. "Nice to meet you, too."

He released my hand and stepped away from me. "Farrell," Mom said. "Let me show you upstairs to the guest room while Mr. Wells gets your things."

Farrell followed her and left me alone in the kitchen. My knees weakened while lightheadedness soared through me. I forced myself to sit. I had no idea how it was possible, but my life had just gotten more complicated.

CHAPTER *Four*

YOU KNOW THAT FEELING YOU get when someone is secretly looking at you? And you don't want to glance their way because you don't want them to know you can tell? It was like that with Farrell. Normally I wouldn't mind a gorgeous guy checking me out, but this was different. It was like he knew me, or knew a secret about me. And then, for a minute there, I thought he knew about my visions. But that would be impossible. And so I decided to ignore him and focus on my immediate problem: being the new girl at a new school.

My old school back home was small, less than a hundred in my class. Now that I was in a big city like Houston, everything was different. Mom had said there were over nine hundred students in the senior class at Harmony High. I had even looked up the giant tan-bricked, three-story school just two miles away from our new house, and read up on it. The school was four years old and had every extracurricular activity you could imagine. They were also the soccer champs in their division every year since the school opened. It was cool and all, but none of that mattered to me since all I could think about were my visions, my visit with Jan, and now the hot guy who had moved in.

At exactly seven on Monday morning, a car horn blared out front—Infiniti. I had texted her about Farrell the night before. She had a ton of questions, but I had no answers. I could only tell her the basics—that he was hot, tall, blond, and had green eyes. That was all I knew, and that was all she cared about.

When we got in the car, the smell of weed, coffee, and perfume assaulted me. The windows were cracked, but I rolled mine down all the way.

"Oops, sorry," Infiniti said, taking a perfume bottle out of her purse and giving it a few squirts. She looked over her shoulder at Farrell in the back seat. "So, you're the new roomie?"

"Yes, I'm Farrell Walker. Nice to meet you."

"Very, very nice to meet you," she said with smile. "I'm Infiniti Clausman." She turned back around and mouthed the word "wow" at me. I hoped he didn't see.

She put her black Mustang in gear and hauled out of the neighborhood. A little kid at the corner bus stop flipped her off, yelling at her to slow down.

"Infiniti, what the hell?" I asked.

"I had to do this stupid report over the Thanksgiving break for extra credit, and I forgot to email it to my teacher last night. If I can get there in time, I can hand it in before first period. Otherwise, I'm screwed."

We got to school in less than five minutes. She screeched to a halt in the nearest parking spot and took off. "See y'all here after school," she hollered over her shoulder as she ran to the building.

"Your friend is quite interesting," Farrell said.

"I know."

When we walked through the double glass doors, every nearby girl stopped and stared at Farrell. I had no claim to him, but a pang of jealousy struck me anyway. I pushed it aside and took out my schedule. Farrell didn't have his yet.

"You know where you're going?" he asked.

Bodies bustled all about us, and the nearby stairwell was crowded with people making their way to class. Luckily, Infiniti had looked over my classes and told me where to go. Unfortunately, I didn't have any classes with her. "Sorta. You?"

Farrell glanced down the hall. "I need to go to the office and get my schedule."

The first bell rang with a blast, jarring me a little. "Maybe we'll have some classes together," I offered.

He nodded. "Maybe."

For some reason I didn't want to leave him, but why? I didn't even know him. Maybe it was because we were both new and thrust into a new school against our will because of our parents and their stupid jobs. Or maybe it was the knowing way he looked at me. I wasn't sure, but it made me uncomfortable. "See ya, Farrell."

"See ya."

There were about twenty students in my first period English class. Infiniti had told me that Veronica was in most of my classes, and sure enough, there she was. She sat in the back row, her hair perfectly combed and her face ready for a photo shoot. I took a seat near the front and pulled out a book.

The teacher breezed in right before the tardy bell. Tall and thin with long, red hair pulled back in a ponytail and blunt bangs that formed a perfect line along the middle of her forehead; she looked more like a model than a teacher. She wore dark pants, black boots, a white shirt, and a long- sleeved black jacket.

After she entered the room, Trent slipped in behind her. He looked better than I remembered — tan and muscular with eyes so blue they sparkled like jewels. His shirt was wrinkled, his jeans torn and faded, much more so than the average guy. He was either in a huge rush, or didn't care about what he wore, which I kinda liked. He spotted me right away, and sat in the desk next to mine.

The teacher went up to the chalkboard. She wrote her name in a fancy cursive, "Ms. Ryken." She was new, too? What were the odds?

"Class, my name is Ms. Ryken. I'm your new English teacher. Your former teacher has taken a leave of absence." She began handing out slips of paper. "The time is here for your follow-up meetings with your academic advisors. On these slips of paper is the name of your advisor and the date and time of your appointment. I recommend you take this seriously and be on time, prepared to talk about your futures, especially since — " She stopped and focused on me. "The deadline is near."

Chattering excitement burst through the

room, while my stomach twisted. Why did she stare at me? I didn't know and I didn't care. I had already picked my school and submitted my application. I was going back home to Northwest Michigan College in Traverse City, and nobody could stop me.

Ms. Ryken dropped my paper on my desk. I wasn't even going to open it, except she nodded at me. When I looked at the paper, I saw her name. So she wasn't just my new English teacher, she was also my academic advisor, and our meeting was set for tomorrow after school. Little did she know I had no intention of going.

"You will be there, Ms. Wells." Her eyes narrowed on me, her eyebrow slightly raised. "Correct?" She glanced at the clipboard in her hands. "Especially since you're a new student."

How could she tell that I was going to ditch? And who cared if I was new? "Yes, I'll be there."

After an hour of a boring lecture on writing style, the bell rang. I swiftly made my way out of Ms. Ryken's room, when Trent came running up beside me.

"Hey, Dominique," he said. "It's me, Trent. I met you at Infiniti's."

Of course I remembered him, but decided to play it cool. "Oh, yeah. That's right. Hi."

"Hi," he said with a smile. "Where ya headed?"

"Calculus."

"Me, too. Can I walk with you?"

"Sure."

He kept his attention on me while responding with a wave to all the hellos and what ups from practically every person we passed. Trent was definitely a popular guy.

"That was some party at Infiniti's. Sorry you had to leave early."

I had no idea what to say. Luckily, he continued. "So, I hear you're from Michigan. Must be pretty different than Texas."

"Yeah, it's different. But everyone's been real nice." Except Veronica, I thought to myself, hoping she wasn't around to see me walking with Trent, even if she did have a new crush like Infiniti said.

As we made our way down the hall, I sensed someone staring at me. I looked around and saw Farrell by the lockers. He started to come my way but stopped when he spotted Trent at my side. His face took on a blank expression before he turned and walked in the opposite direction. I slowed my pace, wondering if I should go after him, when Trent gripped my arm.

"You okay? You're completely zoning out."

"Oh, sorry. My mind went blank for a minute there."

His eyes studied mine. His body inched closer. "Am I boring you?"

My face grew hot, and I hoped it wasn't turning red. "No, no, nothing like that."

The bell rang and not a moment too soon. "Come on," he said with a grin, taking my hand and pulling me into the next open door and our second period class. A big group came in right behind us. I took the last empty seat near the front, forcing Trent to go to the back. As I sat there, I kept replaying the look on Farrell's face when he saw me with Trent, and I didn't understand it. Nothing made sense since moving here, and all I wanted to do was escape my life.

The day crawled by and I only saw Infiniti at lunch. We sat together along with Veronica and Billy, Veronica's new boyfriend. Short and stocky with bright, red hair and freckles, he laughed and joked the entire lunch. I couldn't see fake Veronica with him at all, but I was glad she had found someone new. As for Farrell, I didn't see him again the entire day. And Trent, well, he was in all of my classes.

When the final bell rang at the end of the day, relief washed over me because I had survived my first day as the new girl. I grabbed my stuff and made my way to the parking lot and Infiniti's car. There was no sign of Farrell. I started twisting my hair, worried he wouldn't show, when I stopped and lowered my hands.

Why was I worrying about Farrell?

"Where's your hot roomie?" Infiniti asked, coming over to me while smacking a wad of gum.

Before I could answer, Farrell came up.

"There you are," Infiniti said. "Let's get outta here."

He avoided eye contact with me. "You all go on. I need to go back to the office. Fill out some more paperwork."

I couldn't help but think he was trying to get away from me after seeing me with Trent in the hall. But why would he even care who I talked to?

"How will you get home?" I asked.

"I'll figure it out, it's not far."

"I'll see you later, then."

Infiniti and I watched him make his way through the parking lot and back to the school.

"Holy shit, can I move in with you?" Infiniti asked, leaning against her car. "Just for a little while? I mean, he is H-O-T. The whole school was talking about him, you know. How can you stand it?"

"He's hot and all, but he doesn't talk much." I thought back to how he looked at me when we met, like he recognized me or something, and how he looked at me when he saw me with Trent, his face covered in disappointment.

"Ooh, the strong, silent type," Infiniti said. "I like that."

Infiniti sped out of the school parking lot. She talked the whole way to my house—about what I had no idea. All I could think about was Farrell. He would be staying with me for who knows how long, and I didn't know if I could live with a gorgeous guy who also freaked me out a little.

When I got home, I put my backpack in the kitchen and made my way to the fluffy, white couch in the living room. While I wasn't too crazy about the exterior of our generic, red-brick house, I loved the inside. The main room was big and open with tall windows that lined the back wall and looked out over a lush, shrub-filled backyard. Mom had the room painted a soft and soothing pale green, and the floors were a dark wood.

Our furniture fit perfectly in the space, even the large black armoire Dad had sanded and stained himself. Instead of a TV, Dad put shelves inside for his collection of rocks and fossils from his various expeditions. There were also a few pictures. One of them was of my mom and dad with some college friends. They stood in front of a cabin they went to every summer, arms linked, and faces smiling. I couldn't remember the last time I had seen my parents smile like that.

The room was separated from the kitchen by a double-sided fireplace. Back home the leaves had fallen, the air had cooled, and frost covered the ground. Here, it was still warm, and every tree hung on to its coverings. I wondered if it would ever get cold enough to even need the fireplace.

My eyelids grew heavy, and I decided to stretch out on the couch for a while. My mind drifted, and I was on the verge of sleep when I found myself standing in the same red desert. Heat wrapped around me, a hollow silence filled my ears, and I found it hard to breathe. For a moment, I wondered if I was even alive, but my hand on my chest detected my heart's vibrating rhythm. At least I wasn't dead, even though it felt like death surrounded me.

When I brought my hands down, I was surprised to see I was clutching a long, white feather. My eyes fixed on the plume, my hand opening to expose it fully. It was beautiful— a crisp white with hues of yellow and gold at the edges—and I thought I recognized it, like I had seen it before. Afraid to drop it, I tightened my grip, panic seizing me. My eyes darted around to make sure I was alone. After scanning the area, I brought my attention back to the feather. I gasped. It had escaped my grip and floated down to the red dirt. I watched it drift back and forth in slow motion, my entire body stuck on pause. When the feather reached the crimson ground, white light illuminated from it, like a glowing ribbon reaching up toward me before fading away. The feather looked lifeless, out of place. I should've held on tighter. I shouldn't have let go.

Guilt consumed me.

After what seemed like a few minutes, a sharp pain shot through me at the nape of my neck. This time I sensed a dark and heavy presence behind me. I froze with fear. I knew the presence, and I hated it. Dread filled me, sending slow-moving shivers up my legs that washed over me like deadly ripples of water desperate to drown the life right out of me.

Something horrible was about to happen.

My heart pounded through my ears. The fine hairs all over my body stood on edge. Then, an unspoken thought filled my head.

You belong to me. And I'm going to find you.

Pain shot through the back of my neck. It pulsed through my body like a burst of wild electricity. I stumbled about and slammed my hands over the source of my pain, thinking that would somehow end my torment, but it didn't. I shook my head and blinked, desperately trying to snap myself out of the vision, when I noticed the feather at my feet was gone. In its place swirled a thick, black mist.

Panic cut through my agony. I started screaming, the name Farrell instinctively coming out of my mouth.

"Farrell! Help me!"

CHAPTER
Five

FARRELL'S FACE APPEARED IN FRONT of mine, his hands on my arms as he jostled me away from my vision and back to reality. "Dominique!"

Disoriented and embarrassed, I scooted away from him. I had dozed off only for a few minutes, but it seemed much longer. Sitting up all the way, I took in my surroundings. I was on the couch, but I had just been in that red desert. The heat still lingered on my skin while the pain continued throbbing at the back of my neck. But why did I call out for Farrell? And more importantly, how did he know?

"What time is it?"

He checked his watch. "Three thirty."

Farrell studied me for a moment before backing away. "When I came in, you were having a nightmare."

I thought of the first time I had seen the red desert. It was two nights ago at Infiniti's party, and then I saw it again when I got home. It was like I was dreaming, but I wasn't because my dad

39

had said my eyes were open.

"So I was dreaming? With my eyes closed?"

He hesitated. "Yes, you were dreaming. But your eyes were open."

My hand went to the burning sensation at the back of my neck. What the hell was happening? And why me?

"Dominique, what is it?" he asked. "If there's something going on, you can tell me." He touched my hand, and the feeling of lightheadedness returned. "Maybe I can help you."

Maybe I *could* tell him. After all, I needed someone to confide in. "Well, there is something going on, I guess." I heard the garage door open, and I added quickly, "Can you come to my room tonight after everyone's asleep?" My heart pounded as I waited for his answer, hoping he'd say yes, but afraid he'd say no.

He nodded, his eyes searching mine, his face filled with concern. He squeezed my hand, and a burst of *déjà vu* shot through me. I had been in this situation before, with Farrell, having this conversation. As if he sensed it too, he pulled his hand away and increased the distance between us.

Speechless and confused, I got up and went to the bathroom. I stood there for a moment, my mind processing the emotions running through me—fear, anxiety, but mostly familiarity. But how? As I stood there, I heard someone enter the house.

"Where's Dominique?" I heard my mom say.

"In the bathroom," Farrell replied.

I couldn't stay locked away forever, and I

knew the longer I waited, the harder it would be to come out. I splashed cool water on my face, when the birthmark at the back of my neck sprang to mind. Was the pain somehow connected to the mark? I pulled my hair to the side and looked at the back of my neck through mirror. It looked fine. So what was happening to me? I took a deep breath, exited the bathroom, and walked to the kitchen, pretending nothing had happened while my mind raced. I busied myself with putting groceries away and stayed as far away from Farrell as I could without being obvious. With the last item in its place, my phone beeped. It was Infiniti, texting me to come over.

I left the house and headed down the dark street. My thoughts took me to the vision and how Farrell had showed up when I needed him. I rubbed my hands together, my fingertips still tingling from his touch, when I crashed into someone.

"Hey!" Infiniti called out.

"Oh, crap!" I said, reaching down for Infiniti who had tumbled to the sidewalk. "I'm so sorry."

Infiniti laughed. "What the heck!"

"I didn't see you," I said, trying not to laugh too hard until I knew she was okay.

"No shit," she said, raising herself up and dusting off her shorts. "Well, I've got some news that might knock you on your ass."

"Yeah? What?"

"It's Trent."

My heart skipped a beat. "Trent?"

"Yep, Trent. He texted me asking for your number." She flashed her phone at me, showing me the message.

"Whoa," I whispered.

"Want me to give it to him?"

My hand shot up to my hair, my fingers twisting the strands into a rope-like shape. "I don't know. What about Veronica?"

"They're over. Besides, she and Billy Weber are a legit item now."

I had met Billy at lunch and really liked him. It seemed like Veronica did, too. She couldn't keep her hands off him. "Really?"

"Really. And that makes Trent fair game." She waved her phone in front of my face. "So... what do you want to do?"

The first thing I thought about was Farrell. There was something about him that I was drawn to, but he made me nervous. Trent? He was fun and exciting. Then I thought of my visions. Crazy people have visions. Maybe I needed to see a doctor, take drugs. Or maybe I needed a distraction, like Trent.

"Uh, hello," Infiniti said. "He's asking for your number, not a marriage proposal!"

A nervous laugh escaped my lips. "You're right. I tend to over think things sometimes." I rubbed my hands on my jeans. "Why not, right?"

"Exactly," she said with a grin, texting him my number. "There," she said. "It's done."

I ANXIOUSLY WAITED FOR TRENT to text me, and for Farrell to show up later that night. To pass the time, I studied my room. An oversized window with an arched top filled one of the walls. From my bed I could see the moon peek through the top branches of the oak tree outside. My gaze then drifted to my bare, light blue walls. I had initially planned to hang some of my things, but decided against it. This place would never be home to me, so why pretend like it was?

Finally, at almost eleven, Farrell showed up at my open door.

"Hey," he said. His hair was wet from his shower, and his T-shirt clung to his still damp body. I tried my best not to stare at his chest, and forced myself to focus on his face. Maybe having him come to my room was a bad idea.

"Come in," I said. A nervous flutter entered my stomach as he took a seat on the oversized chair in the corner. I took the blanket at the foot of my bed and wrapped it around my shoulders. Neither of us spoke for a while.

"How was your first day?" I asked, recalling the look on his face when he saw me walking with Trent.

"It was fine," he said. "And it looks like we don't have any classes together."

"I figured."

He leaned forward. "So…" He ran his fingers through his hair. "Do you want to talk? Tell me about your dream maybe?"

Instead of telling him about my dream, something else popped in my mind—Jan. "Do you know anything about numerology and soul lives?"

I half-expected him to laugh or say something funny, but he didn't. Instead, he studied me. His steady and quiet demeanor told me he'd give me some sort of practical answer that would make me feel better. At least, that's what I hoped.

"Well, as I understand it, there are many different theories on what happens when you die. As far as numerology goes, there is a theory that everyone has nine soul lives. Every time you come back you should be closer to fulfilling your purpose—or something like that. Why do you ask?"

"Infiniti took me to a neighbor's house down the street, a lady named Jan. She used a mathematical formula to figure out our soul lives. I'm a nine."

"What does it mean to be a nine?"

"It means I have no more time. This is my final life. Life number nine." I thought I detected a hint of vanilla as Jan's words to get it right this time repeated in my head. I studied Farrell's face and waited for him to tell me I was being stupid. He didn't say that.

"Dominique, you can't worry about something you don't understand. Numerology is only a theory. All we can do is make the most of what we've got and live for today, not tomorrow."

"You're right." I wanted to cry, but stopped myself. "But I don't fit in here. It's like I don't belong. Even my friends back home have moved on without me. And, well, just so you know, I might even be going a little crazy," I said with a pitiful laugh, surprised at how open I was being.

He scooted up to the edge of his seat and leaned close to me. "Dominique, you're stronger than you think. And even though we haven't known each other long, I can tell you're not crazy."

I didn't feel very strong, but the calm and confident tone of his voice strengthened me. "Thanks, Farrell."

He got up to leave my room when I stopped him. "You know, I haven't been that friendly."

He sat back down. "What do you mean?"

I wanted to know if maybe we had met before, or if he had seen me somewhere. There had to be a reason why I thought I knew him. "Well, I haven't even asked you about yourself. I mean, I'm stuck in this city against my will, and now you're stuck in this house with a lunatic." I couldn't help but wonder if he was as miserable as me.

"We've already established you're not crazy, right?"

"Right," I mumbled, but not believing it.

"And as for being here, it's normal for me. My parents travel a lot for work, so I'm used to it."

"So they're geologists like my mom and dad?"

"Yes, and they're off on an expedition somewhere in Europe."

My parents had never both left me for work, though my dad did travel a lot. I still found it hard to believe that one of his projects led us to Houston. But here we were.

"So you're not from Houston either?" I asked.

"I guess you could say, with all my family travels, I'm from everywhere. Now I'm here."

How strange to be from everywhere. But then again, Farrell did seem different. Maybe that was it. Maybe he was just worldly. He got up and lingered for a moment at my door.

45

"Well, good night," he said. "I'll be right next door if you need anything."

They say people have multiple dreams when they sleep, but if so, I never remember mine. But when Farrell left my room and I finally dozed off, I had dreams I remembered. They were flooded with him. And each time I dreamed of him, he said the same thing.

"I'm here for you."

Trent texted me off and on the next day. He texted about lunch, about class, and even the weather, putting a permanent smile on my face. And then, as if mustering up his courage, he finally asked me out. I didn't answer because I wasn't sure what was happening to me, and I didn't want to bring some nice, normal guy into my messed-up life. That wouldn't be fair. But when I went to Infiniti's after school to hang out, Trent and his text messages came up.

"What? He asked you out for tonight and you're ignoring him?" She threw a couch pillow at me. "After texting him all day!"

Saying it like that made me feel like crap. "No! I mean, I guess I am." I threw the pillow back at her. "I don't need a boyfriend right now. That's all."

She stuffed her face with a handful of hot Cheetos and downed them with root beer. "Let's go over this for a moment, shall we?" She criss-crossed her legs, yoga style, and gave me a serious look. "He's the most popular guy at our school. He has top grades. He's our best soccer player by the way, and he's totally into you and you don't want anything to do with him. Does that sum it up?"

"I guess so."

She narrowed her eyes at me. "Oh, I get it. You're interested in someone else, aren't you? Maybe some ultra- gorgeous hottie living under your roof?"

The thought of Farrell gave me an odd yet warm tremor, but something told me not to go there, that it wasn't right. "No. Farrell is not the problem."

"Shit, I can't believe I'm going to say this because I'll probably lose you like I lost Veronica to Billy, but you're being an idiot!"

I stared at Trent's text. Infiniti was right; I was being an idiot. I mean, why not go out with him? What could it hurt? "Fine. You're right. I'll go."

Opening up my messages, I stared at his last text then replied, "Sure, how's 7?"

He texted back right away. "K, will pick u up. 2 story corner house on Infiniti's street, right?"

"Yep. 9002."

I placed my phone face down on my lap and blew out. "He's coming to get me at seven." I muttered mostly to myself, "Hope I'm doing the right thing."

Infiniti put her Cheetos bag and root beer on the coffee table. Her eyes went wide. "Wanna consult the spirits? We can use the Ouija board."

I had completely forgotten about the Ouija board I had seen there earlier. "I don't know, Infiniti. Stuff like that freaks me out."

"It's totally cool. I use the board all the time. Even my mom uses it."

My palms started to get sweaty. What if I saw the red desert again? Or encountered that dark presence from my vision? Or what if something worse happened?

"You know you wanna! I can see it in your eyes!" Infiniti said. "And, you'll get answers. I promise."

Answers… I definitely needed answers. "Fine, just this once. But you have to promise not to tell anyone. Okay?"

She clapped her hands. "Deal!" She turned off the lights and closed the blinds and curtains. She got the game from the other room, slid the board out of the box, and placed it on the coffee table. I sat on one side, and she sat on the other.

"Have you ever played before?" she asked.

"Once, a few years ago at a party, but it didn't work."

"The board always works for me." She cracked her knuckles. "Just follow my lead."

I nodded, letting her take charge while I concentrated on following her moves. She took a series of deep breaths and placed her fingertips on the pointer in the middle of the board. I did the same. As soon as my fingers touched the pointer, my vision snapped to the red desert, and then back to Infiniti's house. My skin tingled with panic. My hands trembled. I tried to steady them, but found it difficult.

"Whoa, you're pale as shit," she said. "Want to stop?"

My body wanted to get up and run, but my mind said to stay, to get some answers. I closed my eyes. When I opened them, I stared at her, waiting for the red desert to reappear, but it didn't.

"I'm all right. Let's keep going."

"Relax," she said soothingly.

"Okay," I said, breathing in deep. Even though my hands had stilled, my heart drummed out of control.

"Do you believe in the power of the board?" she asked me.

"Yes," I said with a gulp. If it meant my visions would go away and I could be normal again, I was willing to believe in anything.

"Open yourself to the spirits," she whispered. "Remove any doubt."

I did my best to clear my mind and continued taking slow and steady breaths. She studied my face, gave a nod, and then closed her eyes. "Good spirits. Connect with me and my friend, Dominique. Give us insight into these matters where we need your guidance."

After a moment, the pointer started moving by itself, our fingertips barely making contact.

She opened her eyes. "I'll go first," she whispered.

"Okay," I said, glad for her to take control.

"Is there a spirit here?"

The pointer went to YES.

"Are you a good spirit?" she asked.

YES.

"Do you know me and Dominique?"

YES.

NO.

Was the board confused?

"Do you know me?" Infiniti asked.

NO.

"Do you know my friend, Dominique?"

YES.

The answer stunned me, gripping me with panic, each hair on my head tingling. Sunlight streaked through the closed blinds and passed right over the board. For a minute there, I thought I saw a hazy, gray vapor hovering over our hands, but it faded away when the ray of light disappeared. Dust—it had to have been dust in the air. As much as I wanted to stop playing, I kept my fingertips planted on the pointer, my desire to know more outweighing my growing fear.

"Who are you?" she asked.

The pointer hesitated for a while, making small circular movements over the letters, stopping until it spelled, F-R-I-E-N-D.

I stared at Infiniti, my mouth open in complete disbelief, the panic inside me growing stronger. I pushed it aside, determined to figure out what was happening to me.

"Will you please answer my friend Dominique's questions?"

YES.

"Go ahead," Infiniti whispered to me.

There was a lot I wanted to know, but where to start and what to ask? I thought for a moment before I began.

"How do you know me?" I asked.

The pointer circled and circled, pulling our fingertips and arms every which way, like it didn't know how to answer. Then, slowly, it spelled: F-O-R-E-V-E-R.

My eyes grew wide, and so did Infiniti's.

"Are you saying you've known me... forever?"

YES.

"I don't understand."

Again the board spelled: F-O-R-E-V-E-R.

"Do you know about the—" I hesitated, afraid to ask about my visions in front of Infiniti, but I had to. "Red desert?" Infiniti's eyes almost popped out of her head.

YES. NO. YES. NO.

The board seemed confused again. Every molecule in my body filled with fear. I wanted to ask about my soul life and my visions when my brain flooded with Farrell—the spark when his hand touched mine, the lightheadedness that followed, the way I thought I knew him.

"Is there something I need to know about... Farrell?"

The pointer went back and forth between YES and NO, then stopped.

Slowly it spelled: N-O-T-F-A-R-R-E-L-L.

The pointer paused, then circled between YES and NO. What? It didn't want to answer questions about Farrell? But why? Did it have something to do with the way he made me feel? Was there some sort of dangerous secret about him?

Infiniti blurted out, "What do you mean 'not Farrell?' If we want to know about him, you must answer."

Again the pointer spelled, a little quicker this time: N-O-T-F-A-R-R-E-L-L.

Why couldn't I ask about Farrell? My stomach twisted into a giant knot. If I couldn't ask about Farrell, then what should I ask about?

"Am I…in some sort of…danger?"

The pointer shot to YES so quickly that neither one of us had our fingers on it.

Infiniti clutched her hands to her chest. "We need to stop."

Her face was so white her black hair stood out in sharp contrast. If she wanted to quit playing, there had to be a good reason. "Okay, let's stop."

As the words escaped my lips, a gust of wind swept through the room. The pointer shot across the board to NO.

"The spirit has changed," Infiniti said. She backed away from the board like her life depended on it.

I scooted away, too, but kept my eyes on the board. I bit my bottom lip when all of a sudden the pointer started moving all by itself in crazy circles. It stopped and shot across the board, stopping over the letters so quickly that it took me a while to make out the message it spelled over and over:

Y-O-U-M-A-R-K-E-D.
Y-O-U-M-A-R-K-E-D.
Y-O-U-M-A-R-K-E-D.
Y-O-U-M-A-R-K-E-D.

Darkness blanketed the room. Every glimmer of daylight erased. Infiniti let out a high-pitched scream. She bolted for the back door. It wouldn't budge. There was no way out. We were trapped. My heart echoed her pounding. My legs froze. Shivers covered my body. A strange eeriness filled the room. I knew this feeling. I knew it was coming. And it did. The red landscape flashed before me. I blinked, and I was back in the den. Another blink—I was back in the desert. My vision flashed in and out of my reality so fast I had no idea where I was. I tried to focus on one image, but neither one would hold.

My head began to spin. My legs weakened. I tried to steady myself when a blast of cutting pain pierced through the back of my neck, like someone had rammed a hot poker right through me. My hands slammed over the spot. I opened my mouth to scream, but nothing came out.

Shadowy movement caught my eye. A dark, black mist trickled out of the board, like the haze in my vision when I saw the feather, but this time it was real. The warm vapor poured onto the floor, swirling around my ankles. Blasting brushes of heat and grit scraped against my skin. As it swept up my legs, it tightened, like giant hands grasping me, holding me in place.

There was nothing I could do. It had me. And then, an image of my parents appeared before me. "You need to call for Farrell," Mom urged. "Now! Hurry!"

I stretched out my hands, but they faded away. Mom's words echoed in my head. I turned all my thoughts to Farrell.

Farrell! Farrell! Farrell!

The house shook with tremendous force. An explosive thunder filled the air. I crashed to my knees. A flashing blast of light illuminated the house with blinding intensity. Everything went white. My head spun. My body burned. Farrell appeared before me. He was so close I could feel his breath on my face.

I wanted to scream out, tell him that it had me, but I couldn't.

I was dying.

CHAPTER *Seven*

My eyes opened to a dim, fluorescent light over-head. I rubbed my head, confused about my whereabouts, my brain fuzzy and stuck on slow motion. After a few seconds, I began to make out my surroundings. I lay on a bed in a room with white walls, the smell of hand sanitizer and alcohol overpowering me. A steady beeping sounded. An IV had been inserted in my hand.

I was in a hospital room. But what was I doing here?

Mom and Dad sat across from me on a small blue couch, leaning on each other. They were fast asleep. I studied them for the first time in a long while. Mom and I looked exactly alike, except for the eyes. Hers were bright green, while mine were olive-colored. Dad's eyes were also bright green, but instead of brown hair like me and mom, his was blond.

I wanted to wake them up, find out what I was doing here, but my brain wasn't connecting with my mouth.

After a moment, I sensed someone at my side. Turning, I saw Farrell. He sat in a chair by my bed. His bloodshot eyes and messy hair sent a panic through me. What had happened? And why was Farrell here? Fear cascaded throughout my body.

"You've been in the hospital for two days with a severe concussion," he explained. "But you're fine now."

What? Then, like a switch being flipped, memories flooded my awareness. I remembered Infiniti, the Ouija board, the mist, the explosion, and the white light. Terrified, I tried to sit up. Farrell gripped my shoulders and held me down.

"It's coming for me! It's coming for me!" I yelled so hard my throat hurt. "Let me go!"

Mom and Dad jumped up and rushed over to me. "Dominique, stop," Dad said. "Nobody is coming for you."

"You're safe now," Farrell added.

Farrell's words penetrated through. I was safe now? How could he know unless— "You…" I muttered. "You were there, weren't you?" I recalled the image of his face in front of mine, surrounded by the bright, white light. "It was all… real?"

"Yes," he nodded.

"Oh, my God," I whispered. Tears filled my eyes and slipped out onto my cheeks because I knew, without a doubt, that I was crazy.

Mom wiped them away. "Dominique, we'll tell you everything, but not here. You're being released tomorrow. We can talk then. Okay?"

We? So they knew what had happened, too? I bit my lip, trying not to come completely unglued, when Farrell took my hands. A warm peace filled me.

"You're safe," he said. "I'm right here."

I'm right here… He had said those words to me before. But where? And when?

"Trust me," he added.

He kept his hands wrapped around mine while I drifted back to sleep.

WHEN I WAS FINALLY RELEASED from the hospital, I started asking questions as soon as we got in the car. "I want to know what the hell happened at Infiniti's. And I want the truth. Right now."

Farrell shifted in his seat. "Well," he said. "I told the firemen and the EMTs that I had seen a tornado touch down by Infiniti's, and when I went into the house I found you and Infiniti knocked out."

A tornado? Was he for real?

He cleared his throat. "And then—"

"Stop!" I blurted. "There was no tornado!"

"Dominique," Mom explained in her soothing parental voice that irritated the hell out of me. "Farrell is telling you what he reported so you can know the story."

Crossing my arms, I guessed it made sense to have a story because who in their right mind would believe what really happened when I hardly believed it myself? An Ouija board spirit attacking me and Infiniti? Farrell appearing in a burst of white light? None of it made any sense.

"Fine, okay, I know the story. Now I want real

answers."

When we got inside, I sat on the couch and held my hands together on my lap, my fingers digging into my skin, a lump forming in my throat. Mom and Dad stood in front of me. Farrell came and sat by my side. My face began to flush. "Farrell, you can go upstairs. This doesn't concern you."

"He needs to be here for this," Mom said.

I jumped to my feet. "Are you kidding me? He's a total stranger. He doesn't even know us!"

"Dominique, please. Hear us out," Dad pleaded.

"No! You hear me out! You brought me to this stupid city, and I hate it here! Everything about this place sucks, and now, because of you, I'm crazy!" Tears trickled down my face, and I wiped them away. "Okay? Fucking crazy! And it's all your fault!"

I bit my lip because I regretted my words, but they were out already. Besides, they needed to know how pissed I was.

Dad paced the room. "You have every right to be upset, Dominique. We never meant for any of this to happen."

I didn't even notice Farrell at my side until he took my hand. A soft tingle entered my body. "Dominique, I told you. You're not crazy."

My head began to swoon. My knees buckled. Every time I was near Farrell, a funny feeling came over me. Sometimes it was a subtle dizziness, other times a tingle throughout my body, but always the feeling warmed me. Calmed me. And seemed so natural and familiar.

"What are you doing to me?" I whispered.

"He's helping," Dad said. "Please, both of you. Sit."

Farrell continued holding my hand, and together we sat on the couch. My mind raced. Helping with what?

"Dominique," Dad said, rubbing his face. "I want you to please listen without interrupting. What I'm about to say is important."

My stomach tightened. I sucked in my breath, waiting for a punch to the gut.

"The world we know today hasn't always been like this." He glanced at Mom. "This entire world, this planet as we know it, is called by some as New Earth, but before the birth of mankind, it was different. We call that world, the world before, the Old Earth. The Old Earth was inhabited by beings called Transhumans, beings that looked like you and me, but had the ability to control the energy within them and around them—almost like superpowers."

"No, no, no," I whispered out loud but mostly to myself. "You guys can't be crazy, too. You can't." My throat ached from the lump blocking my tears, but I didn't want to cry, didn't want them to know how badly I needed them to be sane.

"Dominique, nobody is crazy," Mom said. "Now please, let your father finish."

Dad went on. "When the New Earth was born, the Transhumans made a pact not to interfere with its history, but some broke the pact when mankind appeared. Instead of working for good, they turned, and worked for evil by corrupting the weak souls on New Earth. We call these Transhumans the Tainted. Those who honored the pact and protected mankind later became known as the Pure."

Transhumans? The Pure? The Tainted? None of it made any sense. "Why are you telling me this? And what does it have to do with me?" Panic soared through my veins because I knew it had everything to do with me. The visions, the searing pain at the back of my neck, the presence that tried to get me when we played the Ouija board... everything pointed to me.

"Dominique," Mom said. "Your father, Farrell, and I are Pures. And you, my daughter, are in grave danger."

I shook my head, fighting back the tears that bubbled beneath the surface. My watery eyes fixed on Mom. "What do you mean?" My voice trembled, and I forced myself not to lose it. Farrell squeezed my hand. His grip grounded me, but at the same time freaked me out. I mean who the hell was he? He released his hold and sat back a little.

Did he know my thoughts?

"Dominique," Mom said. "There's more we need to tell you. But first, you must tell us what happened at Infiniti's."

My blood boiled. They wanted me to tell them everything? After everything they'd kept from me? "No!" I rose to my feet, my hands curled up into fists at my side. I couldn't look at them anymore, so I directed my gaze to the window instead, to the backyard that littered with leaves. Wait, leaves? Had the weather finally changed? I closed my eyes, picturing Elk Rapids in December. All the trees, except for the pines, would've dropped their leaves by now. The ground covered in snow. That's when I realized how much I missed winter and needed cool air on my skin. More importantly, I needed to get away. I strode to the back door, refusing to look back.

"I'm leaving. Don't follow me."

Cold air swept across my face as I hurried out the back gate, across the street, and to the lake. Mom's words played over and over in my head. *Your father, Farrell, and I are Pures. And you, my daughter, are in grave danger.*

I found a bench facing the lake and sat, crossing my shivering arms. Everything that had happened to me since moving flashed through my mind. I tried to organize the events, when it hit me. The cards. It all started with the cards at Infiniti's. That's when all the weird stuff started happening. Now I was in grave danger…

A drop of water landed on my cheek. The sky had filled with thick, gray clouds and I couldn't help but think the weather reflected my emotions. I wrapped my arms tighter around my body, the scent of rain all around me. I didn't mind the rain or the cold; they reminded me of Elk Rapids. And so I sat while droplets of rain came down more steadily.

I crossed my arms tighter, my teeth chattering. I wasn't sure I could last out here much longer when I heard the steady pounding of a jogger on the nearby gravel path. I raised my shoulders and lowered my head, in case it was Farrell coming to get me.

"Dominique? Is that you?"

I turned to find Trent. He wore black sweat pants with gaping holes at the knees, and a faded white sweatshirt. "What are you doing out here?" he asked with a smile. "It's about to pour."

"Well, it wasn't raining when I got out here," I said, trying to sound normal.

"Yeah, I know what you mean." He laughed, and then stopped, catching on that something was up. "Can I walk you home or something?"

"No!" I called out. He raised his eyebrows, startled at my quick response. "I mean… no. I can't go there right now."

"Well, why don't you come to my place instead? A massive cold front is rolling in, and that rain's gonna come down any second now."

I wore shorts, a T-shirt, and flip-flops. Goose bumps lined my skin. He was right. I needed to get out of the cold, but what about the danger I was in? I was about to say no when he took my hand.

"Come on, I don't live far."

There was no denying the spark between us. And then I remembered I was supposed to have dinner with him the night of the Ouija board incident.

"I stood you up," I said between chattering teeth. "I'm so sorry."

He laughed and brought me closer. "You're apologizing to me? After being hurt when a tornado touched down on your block?" A cool blast of air brushed past us, carrying with it a hint of clean soap from him that I recognized from Infiniti's party. "You're the most interesting person I know, Dominique." He squeezed my hand, and when he did, Farrell's face popped in my head. Guilt filled me, and I pushed the image aside. "Now come on, let's go to my place before we freeze to death."

Trent led me to his car parked down the street. It was an old, black Camaro. Rust stains spotted the exterior, and a huge crack splashed across the windshield. When he opened the door, I hesitated. What if the black mist that tried to get me through the Ouija board was inside the car? What if it watched me from the tall pines that lined the lake? Shivers cascaded up and down my spine, and my entire body shook.

"Man, you're freezing," Trent said. "I've got a towel in the back."

I lowered myself onto the seat, halfway expecting something to grab me, but nothing happened. Trent leaned over me, reached for a towel from the backseat, and draped it over my legs. He ran to the driver's side, hopped in, and we took off right before the downpour.

The worn, black, leather interior of the car smelled like fresh wax. The floorboards were spotless. "I don't live in Rolling Lakes, but I come and jog in your neighborhood all the time," he explained as he made his way out of my neighborhood into an adjacent one. "I live over here, in Wooded Fork."

The homes were small and old. Some were well-kept and pristine, like little gingerbread houses. Others looked worn and neglected. After several turns, we came to a small one-story, blue, wood-sided house with white shutters and a white picket fence. It oozed with charm, and Christmas decorations.

"Wow," I said. "Your house is beautiful."

"Thanks. I spend a lot of time on it, making it look as nice as possible for my grandmother."

"You do?" I asked, dumbstruck.

"Yeah, when I have time that is. I work at the corner store most nights and weekends when I don't have soccer."

I stared at him in complete wonderment. Here he was, one of the nicest guys I'd ever met, dressed in worn clothes and driving a beat-up old Camaro because he couldn't afford otherwise. I had no idea.

We dashed through the rain to the front door and walked into a small living room with a line of windows at the back of the house. They showcased the now crackling lightning from outside. A warm color palette of cream and beige filled the house, giving it a cozy woodsy feeling. The furnishings were small, dark antiques, and I couldn't help but think it a great house for a hobbit. A slender, medium- sized Christmas tree twinkled in the corner. It didn't display many ornaments, but it was perfect. I hadn't thought of Christmas at all, but here it was, alive in this house.

"Trent, I love your home," I said. And I did, because for some reason I felt safe, as if nothing could happen to me here.

"Let me show you around." He took my hand and led me to the kitchen. "This is the heart of our home. My grandmother spends a lot of time in here making the most delicious food you'll ever have."

Crosses of different sizes and metals lined the buttery yellow walls. An oversized portrait of Jesus hung proudly in the middle. Flanking the shrine were avocado-green appliances that looked like they had come right out of the seventies. A large clear jar filled with orange-colored juice sat on the counter. Trent took a ladle and served two cups. He handed one to me.

"Try this. It's called agua fresca."

I raised the cup to my nose. A sweet, fruity smell made my mouth water. "What's agua fresca?"

He took a drink. "It's fresh fruit juice made with sugar and water. This one is cantaloupe."

I took a small sip. He was right; it was delicious. The freshest fruit drink I'd ever had. "Wow, this is yummy." After a few more sips, I wondered about the rest of his family. "You mentioned your grandmother?"

"Yep, it's just me and my grandmother. My mom and dad died in a car crash when I was eight, and my grandfather died of cancer five years after."

Every shred of fear inside me melted away. All of a sudden, my worries weren't that important anymore. "Trent, I'm so sorry."

He shrugged his shoulders. "It's okay. It was a long time ago."

An awkward silence filled the air, and I didn't know what to say. Luckily, he noticed my still shivering body. "You're still cold. Come on. Let me get you a sweatshirt."

I followed him to his room. When we walked in, I found it neat and orderly, like the inside of his car. He grabbed a white sweatshirt with blue lettering and handed it to me. Rice University. I wondered if he had family that had gone there, or maybe that was where he wanted to go. I slipped it on, and the fresh soapy scent I often smelled from Trent enveloped me.

A simple, dark blue quilt covered his twin-size bed. He had a desk, a nightstand, and a dresser — all dark antiques. On the desk were some books, some pads and pens, and a speaker for his phone. The walls were bare, except for a mirror over his desk. His nightstand held a lamp, alarm clock, and two pictures. I walked to the nightstand to take a closer look.

He sat on the bed. "That's my parents. The other is me with my grandparents."

I picked up the pictures. His parents were young, maybe in their twenties. His mother looked like a movie star. She had long dark hair and exotic features. His dad had messy brown hair and piercing blue eyes, like Trent.

The other picture was Trent and his grandparents. Trent looked about ten. It was interesting to see he hadn't changed at all. His hair was uncombed, his clothes a mess, and he looked so happy.

"That's us at Disneyworld. My grandparents used their savings to take me there. I'll never forget that trip. I didn't find out until later that we went right after my grandfather had been diagnosed with cancer."

He looked away from me, like he didn't want to talk about it. I wanted to say something, but he got out his phone and turned on some music. Airy and ethereal music filled the air, almost dreamlike, the voice of the singer melodic and mysterious. After a moment, Trent sighed and lay down on his back, hands behind his head. Joining him, we stared at the ceiling while the music poured over us.

My thoughts turned to the conversation I had just had with my parents. *And you, my daughter, are in grave danger.* Everything in my body told me to leave, but I ignored the warnings. I wanted to be here with Trent because here I was a normal girl. Not a girl with crazy parents and a crazy guy living in her house.

"What were you doing at the lake?" he asked.

Panic seized me. I brought my hand up to my hair and began twisting. There was no way I could tell him what my parents had said. An old Earth? With a whole race of beings before humans called Transhumans? Pures and Tainted? My life in danger? He'd think me nuts, and I wouldn't blame him.

"I needed to think."

He angled his body closer to mine. Our eyes locked. The soft music encouraged me to want him. The thunder outside and rain on the rooftop forced me closer. He took my hand, untwisting the hair from my fingers.

I stared into his deep, sapphire eyes a moment when my thoughts filled with Farrell. But why? Why did I keep thinking of him? I looked away, avoiding what I thought might be a kiss. He released my hand and sat up. Even though I wanted to be normal and date a normal guy, it wasn't possible. And there was no way I could explain how wrong I was for him.

Trent started to say something when the front door opened. "She's early," he said. Taking my hand, we made our way to the front room.

"*Abuela*," he said. "Are you okay?"

"Yes, *Mijo*, I'm all right. I had Sister Joanne drop me off early. I was tired, and this cold front made my bones ache. I'm an old woman, you know. Besides, I always lose at bingo."

She was a small-framed woman, about eighty, with a round face and perfectly styled, black-dyed hair. She wore green pants and a floral print sweater. A large silver rosary hung from her neck, and she clutched a small red Bible in her hand.

"*Abuela*, this is Dominique. Dominique, this is my grandmother."

I moved forward and noticed her eyes were a cloudy blue. She looked around the room as if searching for me.

"My grandmother can't see," Trent explained in a hushed voice.

"Yes, but I can hear fine," she retorted, raising her index finger.

"I'm Dominique. It's nice to meet you."

Her eyes landed on me. "I can hear where you are, but I can't see you." She peered at Trent. "*Mijo*, can you see her color?"

I must've had a freaked out look on my face because Trent gave my arm a reassuring squeeze. "My grandmother and I can see auras—mine is blue. And no *Abuela*, I can't see Dominique's. Which doesn't mean anything," he offered quickly.

What? They couldn't see my aura?

69

"Yes, but I should be able to see her..." His grandmother's words trailed off. "Oh, never mind. *Mija*, come closer."

She extended her hand for a shake, her fingers twitching ever so slightly. I took it and she squeezed. Her hand was thin, bony, and cold from the outside. "It's nice to meet you, Dominique. Please, call me *Abuela*."

"*Abuela* means grandmother," Trent said.

"And Dominique means belonging to God," his grandmother said.

My mouth opened. I had forgotten that my name meant that. Now I wondered if my name was somehow connected to what was happening to me

"It's nice to meet you, *Abuela*."

She squinted before letting out a long sigh. "Your parents are worried about you."

How could she know that? I stepped away from her, afraid of what she might say next, and feeling guilty that my parents were worrying about me.

"My grandmother sometimes senses things," Trent said. "It's okay. It used to scare me when I was little, but really it's nothing."

I gulped, anxiety shooting through me. "I do need to go. It's late. Plus, your grandmother's probably right about my parents since I didn't tell them where I was going."

Trent placed his hand at the small of my back to usher me out, when his grandmother came up to me. She closed her eyes and took in another deep breath. I braced myself for what she might say.

She opened her cloudy eyes. "*Mija*, what are you doing for Christmas?"

Her question surprised me. "Um, I don't know. We recently moved here, and well, my parents are busy with work."

"*Mija*, you do celebrate Christmas, right?"

"Well, yes, we do. We're just not into it this year for some reason." Of course, I knew the reason. My life was in danger. My parents weren't who I thought they were.

"Well," Trent offered. "If you're not doing anything, how about joining us for dinner and midnight mass Christmas Eve?"

"Midnight mass?"

"Midnight mass is the most sacred mass of the Catholic Church," Trent's grandmother explained. "It's when we celebrate the birth of Jesus Christ, our Savior."

Before I could say no, Trent's grandmother reached out and held my arm. "You must come."

Must? It was an odd word choice. Going with them to a sacred mass probably wasn't a good idea. I was about to say no when her hand tightened around my arm, her grip strong for an old woman.

"Please. You must come with us." Her cloudy blue eyes stared at me without blinking. "It's where the Pures go."

My heartbeat sped up and I let out a small gasp.

"*Abuela*," Trent said. "She probably has plans—"

I cut him off and repeated her words. "It's where the Pures go?"

71

She held me in a death grip. "Yes, *Mija*. The pure of heart."

The room stilled, the thunder stopped. My eyes studied hers before landing on her rosary. That's when I remembered the card I had drawn at Infiniti's.

There are heavenly forces working behind the scenes to help you, even if you don't see results yet.

She was right; I needed to go. "Yes, I think I can go. But I'll need to check with my parents first."

She released my arm, gave a big smile, and stared right at me. "Good."

CHAPTER *Eight*

TRENT DROVE ME HOME IN silence while my mind flooded with his grandmother's every word. She couldn't see my aura, and she wanted me to join them for Christmas Eve mass—where the Pures go. Using that word couldn't have been a coincidence. Could it? If Trent knew the truth about how messed up I was, he'd stay far away from me.

When we got to my house, I opened the door to hop out when Trent put his hand on my knee. "Dominique, if you don't have any plans for Christmas Eve, you're more than welcome to join me and my grandmother. That is, if you want."

I closed the door, glad to stay in his warm car for a little longer. "I do want to go, really, but there's something you should know about me." Wanting to give him some sort of explanation about my life to help him understand me a little, I offered the simplest of explanations. "Moving here has been real hard on me. It's like I'm all alone, and I don't even know who I am anymore.

I mean, I don't even have an aura. That should tell you something about how screwed up I am."

Trent took my hand. "I'm sorry, Dominique. I didn't know you were going through such a hard time. But you're not alone. I know we don't know each other very well, but you've got me. And the whole aura thing, well, it's nothing. Forget about it. Sometimes an aura can't be seen."

I didn't believe him about the aura thing, but I did believe he wanted to be there for me. How could he be so nice? If only I could be normal. Things between us would be different.

"Is there anything else?" he asked.

I thought of being in danger, of the black mist that came after me, of the way Farrell invaded my mind, and now my absent aura. "I don't want to hurt you, that's all."

He brought his hand to my chin and turned my face to him. "Hurt is a part of life. I know hurt, Dominique. But you have to know that it's harder to play it safe than it is to live."

I stared into his deep blue eyes. He did know hurt. He had lost both his parents and then his grandfather. Now he was supporting himself and his grandmother. Life wasn't fair. Not for him, not for me.

Maybe not for anybody.

AFTER CONVINCING TRENT HE DIDN'T have to walk me in, I made my way to the back door. The closer I got there, the thicker my fear. I wasn't worried about Mom and Dad being mad at me for taking off. Instead, I feared the rest of their explanation. I feared knowing more about the danger I was in.

When I walked into the house, I spotted Farrell on the couch. He got up right away, his eyes landing on my sweatshirt: Rice. I had forgotten to give it back to Trent. I crossed my arms against my chest, for some reason guilty for having on another guy's clothes.

"Where are my parents?"

"We're here," Mom answered, walking into the room with Dad at her side. She touched my arm. "Are you okay?"

"Yes," I said, but thinking no. "And I'm ready to hear more. And I want the whole truth. No more lies."

She nodded and took a seat with Dad on the couch. I took the side chair, distancing myself from them. Farrell stayed by the fireplace.

"You guys said you wanted to know what had happened," I said. "Well, it all started at Infiniti's. We played this card game where you ask a question and the card gives you the answer. When I touched the cards—" I hesitated, unsure of how to explain what had happened to me. "I saw a red desert, like I was there, but I wasn't."

Dad closed his eyes. "Describe it."

"It was flat, and everything was red. The sky, the dirt. It was so hot that the air burned my nose and lungs. And everything looked familiar. Like I'd been there before."

Mom's hands went to her mouth. "Dominique, why didn't you tell us?"

"Because I thought I was crazy, Mom! Don't you get it? I thought it was all in my head." I also wanted to say that it was their fault, but I didn't. I couldn't lay that blame on them, no matter how mad I was about everything.

"You saw it again in your room that night, didn't you?" Dad asked.

"Yes, I did. I also saw it two other times."

Dad looked at Mom. "I knew it," he whispered.

"Wait. You knew? Why didn't you tell me! Why didn't you do anything?"

"We couldn't know for sure, Dominique," Dad explained. "But we did do something, we called for Farrell. He is a special Pure, a Walker, assigned to protect you."

"And we were going to tell you," Mom added. "But we didn't know how far ahead of us the Tainted were."

The Tainted… I remembered sensing someone behind me in that red desert. My skin prickled with fear.

"You felt him, didn't you?" Farrell asked. His green eyes were usually tranquil and serene, but now they were stormy and filled with rage. A chill spread through me and I shuddered.

"Yes, I did."

"When?" Farrell asked.

"I was drifting asleep here on this couch, and I found myself in that red desert again. I knew there was a presence behind me. I couldn't see it, but I heard it. It said, 'You belong to me, and I'm going to find you' and then you woke me up. I called to you, without even meaning to, and you came."

My mind shot back to my vision. For a minute, I thought I could smell the dirt from the red desert, thought I could feel the heat invade my nose and lungs.

"A few days later I was at Infiniti's." I remembered the text from Trent asking me to go out. I avoided Farrell's gaze, deciding to keep that part to myself. "We were playing the Ouija board. It was stupid, I know, but I thought the board could give me answers."

"What did you ask it?" Mom said.

"I asked about Farrell. But the board didn't want to talk about him. Then, I asked if I was in danger." I closed my eyes in painful recollection. "It pointed to YES. After that, everything seemed different. Infiniti said the spirit had changed. Then the board spelled 'you marked' over and over."

My hand went to my birthmark, fear flooded my thoughts, and my entire body shook.

"Dominique, it's okay. We don't have to talk about it," Mom said.

"Yes, we do," I demanded. "The same feeling from my visions, that fear and dread, surrounded me until I saw a black mist coming out of the board, coming for me. And then I saw…" The shimmery image of Mom and Dad flashed before my eyes.

"What?" Dad prodded. "What did you see?"

"I saw you, Dad. And Mom. But not really you. It was a vision of you. And Mom, you told me to call for Farrell. And I did. That's when a blinding white light filled the room." I looked at Farrell, recalling his face before mine. "I thought I was dying." The lump in my throat expanded.

Don't cry, I said to myself. *Not now.*

"I'm so sorry, Dominique," Mom said. She walked over and took my hands, kneeling down in front of me. "We're never going to let anything happen to you," she whispered.

Tears rushed to the surface. It took every effort to force them in, and words escaped me. I nodded and squeezed her hands.

"It's time for you to hear the rest," Dad said. "The Tainted and the Pure warred over their role amongst humans. Many innocents died until it was decided to have the fate of their conflict rest on one soul. A marked one; one born unto the Pure. This will be the one who, if taken by the Tainted, will lead to their victory and bring about the Next World, a world filled with darkness, misery, and destruction."

Dad approached me. "It is also said that this marked one will have the ability to defeat the Tainted, and restore peace and order amongst all Transhumans."

Shivering tingles of panic and fear cascaded through my body. "I'm the one," I muttered.

"Yes, you are," Mom confirmed.

I released her hands, not wanting to talk anymore about Transhumans, Pures, and the Tainted. I closed my eyes for a moment, hoping that maybe if I stopped thinking about it, it would all go away when a small hint of vanilla wafted my way. My eyes snapped open, my time at Jan's house springing to mind. "Does all this have something to do with my final soul life?"

Mom, Dad and Farrell stood before me, the three of them so beautiful and striking, all of them with the same green eyes, and now I knew why. They were Pures.

"Yes," Farrell answered. "There are some souls who are given time to complete a task. You are one of those souls. You have been waging this war now for eight lifetimes. So have all those directly linked to your path." He sat next to me. "This is your final life, Dominique. The final battle for the marked one is upon us."

If my heart raced any faster, it would've exploded right out of me. "What about all the other times before? What happened to us?" I asked, afraid to know, but desperate for the answer.

"We do not know what has gone before. It is hidden," Mom explained. "But we do know that you are marked in very life, at the back of your neck. And in every life, we search for a way to remove it by studying ancient scrolls and testaments. Our hope is that by removing the mark, we can save your life. That's why we moved to Houston."

All this time I was pissed at them for bringing me here, angry that Dad spent so much time with his work, but it was all to save me. Everything they had done was for me. Guilt filled me. Then I thought of Farrell. He was special. He was my protector. Maybe he knew something that we didn't.

"Farrell, if you're my walker, sent to help me in each life, then you should know what has happened before, right?"

"No, I cannot see what has gone before. But I do know that I have always been with you."

So that was how I knew him. I had been

with him for eight lifetimes, and now it was our ninth. He had always been with me. My thoughts turned to the red desert, of the way I remembered that place, and how I dreaded it.

"Each time, I die," I whispered, recalling the dark presence and the warning it would find me. "I die in the red desert."

Farrell stood close. "Yes, you do."

CHAPTER *Nine*

I HAD DIED EIGHT TIMES in that red desert. I wanted to run to my room, bury myself under my covers, hide away forever, but something bothered me. My hand went to my birthmark. "Why now? If I'm really this marked one, why am I in danger now?"

Dad looked tired and worn, and I wondered how long it had been since he slept. Days? Months? Years? "Your mother and I have the ability to shield, and we've been shielding you since this all started, hoping to find a way to remove your mark before you were found."

I pictured an invisible bubble surrounding me. Maybe that was why Trent's grandmother couldn't see my aura. My parents had covered it.

"We think," Mom continued, "that playing those cards and the Ouija board weakened our efforts and a bit of your energy was released."

"Wait a minute, so I'm still in danger?" My heart sped up again; my stomach lurched.

"You're not in immediate danger," Dad said.

"We reinforced the shield when you were in the hospital. The Tainted may know you're in Houston, but with the shield in place they can't put a lock on you."

Mom took my hand and held it tight. "We know there are answers here. We simply haven't found them yet, so we can't leave. Houston may be our only hope."

FINALLY, I WAS IN MY room, surrounded by my own private ocean. Although exhausted, I couldn't sleep. My mind raced with everything I had learned. Mom and Dad had said I was safe, but I didn't believe them. The only thing that made me feel better was having Farrell one room away from mine. I wondered if he was asleep. Or maybe he didn't sleep? He was my walker after all, my protector. Even though I knew what that meant, I didn't completely understand it.

After tossing and turning, I stared at the tree branches outside my window. They were stiff, frozen in time. Like me. My body shivered from the cool air that hugged the house and seeped into my room. I sat up and looked at Trent's sweatshirt draped over the chair. I was about to get it, when I heard something.

"Hey."

I yelped, nearly jumping out of my skin. It was Farrell standing at my doorway. "Dominique, I'm sorry. I didn't mean to scare you."

My hands went to my chest, clutching my shirt up to my neck. "Don't do that!"

He smiled. "I heard movement in your room so decided to check on you. Can I come in?"

He heard me sit up? Did he have super hearing or something? "Sure, come in." I turned on my lamp and pulled my comforter up to my chin. My heart fluttered while he sat next to me, his gaze landing for a moment on the sweatshirt still on the chair. That's when I noticed faded marks that streaked from his hands up to his elbows, like old wounds.

"How did that happen?" I asked.

He rubbed his arm. "It's the energy that blasted from the Ouija board when I shut it," he said. "It burned me, but I'm fine."

My hands covered my mouth. "You got that because of me?" Here I was complaining about him, and he had injured himself risking his life for me. "Farrell, I'm so sorry."

"Don't worry. It's nothing. It's almost completely healed anyway."

My mind flashed back to the mist that had come out of the board and swept around my ankles. "That black mist was one of the Tainted?"

"Yes, his name is Tavion. He was about to manifest but hadn't come out all the way."

I reached out and touched his hand. "Thank you, Farrell. You saved my life." My head began to soar. My mind grew fuzzy. I moved my hand away fast.

Farrell took that as is cue to leave. "I'm down the hall if you need me."

When he left my room, I had more questions than answers, so many that my head wanted to explode. Mom and Dad had said that Transhumans were energy beings, but what did that mean? Why was I marked and not somebody else? And how could Farrell protect me this lifetime if in all others I had died? My questions would have to wait for the morning, and it couldn't come soon enough.

MY BODY ACHED WITH FATIGUE when I awoke, letting me know I hadn't gotten enough sleep. I went to the bathroom to splash water on my face. My eyes were puffy and encased in dark circles, my skin pale. I started putting on some makeup so I wouldn't look so awful when my stomach growled. I tried to think of the last thing I'd eaten, but couldn't remember. This wasn't good at all, and I knew I needed to get something in me.

I found Mom and Dad in the kitchen making breakfast. Farrell sat at the table working on a puzzle, something my dad had always done to ease his mind. I grabbed a biscuit, but my stomach knotted. Suddenly the idea of eating made me want to hurl. I put the bread back on the plate and decided to go directly into my questions.

"There are some things I don't understand," I blurted out, not really sure how to ease into a conversation about my death.

Mom sat next to me. "We thought that would be the case."

"I don't get energy beings. What does that mean? How does that work?"

Dad sat on a stool by the kitchen island. "Let me begin with explaining the human brain. There are about a hundred billion neurons in the brain. Each neuron connects to a thousand other neurons. These neurons communicate with each other and transmit information throughout the body. All this information, when added together, forms an electrical discharge, or a nerve impulse."

"Energy," I muttered.

"Yes, energy," Mom repeated. "It propels the body into action. With Transhumans, the neurons work the same, except we have more of them."

"More?"

"At least double," she said. "That's how we're able to do the things we do."

I thought of how Mom and Dad had been shielding me, how Farrell appeared in Infiniti's house when that black mist tried to get me, how he had healed his arm from that blast of energy from Tavion, and how he could hear me in my room from down the hall. They were more than human. For the first time since playing the cards at Infiniti's, I thought I might be okay. Like they could protect me... this time.

"Anything else?" Dad asked.

The smell of sizzling bacon filled the air. Usually I loved bacon, but not today. My twisted stomach couldn't take it. If anything, I needed to get out into the cool air, but I wasn't finished yet.

"Yeah, I've got another question. Why me? Why am I marked and not someone else?"

Mom and Dad fell silent. A myriad of emotions displayed across their faces. Hurt. Worry. Guilt. I braced myself for their answer because it couldn't be good.

"Dominique, the prophecy of the marked one

is ancient," Dad said. "It is said that the marked one will be chosen at random and will be identified by a mark at the nape of the neck." He paused, as if afraid to go on. "A red mark symbolizing the touch of the Tainted."

My hands went to the back of my neck while a fresh wave of horror ran through me.

"Dominique, we don't know why it's you. There is no explanation," Mom said. She reached out for my hand. "We did everything we could to remove the mark, but nothing worked. And then we hoped that somehow your life would be spared, that the Tainted would perhaps not pursue you this time, but they do in each life." Her eyes watered. "Dominique, not a day goes by that your father and I don't agonize over your fate, wondering what we could've done differently to spare you."

Tears filled my eyes. "So my mark can't be removed? Not even with your abilities?"

"There is no way that we know of," Dad said. "Yet."

I wanted to get away and be alone with my thoughts when I realized something. I was their daughter, the offspring of Transhumans, yet I was normal.

"Wait a second. Why am I not like you? I mean, since I'm your daughter, then I should be like you guys, right?" I looked at Mom and Dad, and then Farrell. His eyes met mine before he cast them down. He knew their answer.

"We don't understand either," Dad said.

Great. I was a freak of nature with a death stamp on my body and nobody could save me, not even them.

"We're not going to let anything happen to you," Farrell said. "I promise."

How could he promise me anything when I had died already eight times? How could any of them help me?

Just then the doorbell rang. The timing couldn't have been better.

"I'll get it," I offered, eager to leave the conversation. When I opened the door, I found Infiniti. It had to have been around fifty degrees outside, yet she wore shorts, a sweatshirt, and flip-flops. "Morning! You look… good!" I could tell she was lying because I knew I looked like shit.

"Yeah, right," I said with a laugh.

Infiniti walked in. "Okay, maybe you do look a little out of it, but you've been through a lot. I mean, hell, you got amnesia and a concussion from that tornado. All I got was stupid amnesia. I could've used a few more days off from school."

So she totally believed the tornado story Farrell had made up. Good. I hoped her memory wouldn't return. I started to suggest we go to her house, when I thought of Tavion. My parents had said I was safe, that they had reinforced my shield, but would that extend outside my house? Trent's words echoed in my mind. It's harder to play it safe than it is to live. He was right. I wasn't going to live in fear. Not anymore. I was sick of it.

"Infiniti, can we go to your house?"

"Sure, whatever you want."

She waited at the door while I went to Mom and Dad. "You guys said I was safe, that you had reinforced my shield, right?"

Mom hesitated before answering. "That's right."

She knew exactly what I wanted to do, and she wasn't thrilled. "Well, I'm going to Infiniti's then."

Farrell jumped to his feet, like he didn't want me to leave. Dad stopped him with a wave of his hand. "Go on, Dominique," Dad said. "You should be fine, but if something happens, call for Farrell."

Worry and sadness covered Mom's and Dad's faces. I couldn't leave like that, no matter how mad I was at them and the whole situation.

"Mom, Dad, it's not your fault."

Finally, I had let them off the hook. Now all I could do was hope they'd figure something out—before it was too late.

CHAPTER *Ten*

THE CRISP AIR OUTSIDE RE-ENERGIZED me. The sun shone bright, and the cloudless blue sky stretched out for miles. If winters were like this, then life in Houston couldn't be so bad, unless, of course, someone was trying to kill you.

Infiniti chatted the short walk to her house about the winter break, only two weeks away. She and her mom were going to Breckenridge, Colorado. When she asked about my plans, I said I was staying home and doing nothing, though I thought something different. My plans were to stay alive by avoiding an evil energy being named Tavion, because if I died, the world would be doomed.

And then it dawned on me. If I could tell any-one, it was Infiniti. Something like that probably wouldn't even faze her. But it might put her in danger, so forget that.

As we approached her house, I glanced at Jan's. As we passed, she came out. She wore a long, black coat and held a wooden walking stick in her hand. She nodded at me, and then stood there, staring at us.

"Look, there's Jan," Infiniti said. "Hey, Jan!"

I raised my hand in a silent hello, hoping Infiniti wouldn't want to go over there. Luckily she didn't.

Once we were inside her house, Infiniti grabbed a box of Hostess cupcakes, a giant bag of hot Cheetos, two sodas, and flopped on the couch. Her house looked fine—completely normal. Infiniti had mentioned replacing some windows and blinds from the "tornado," but glancing around you'd never know she and I almost died here. My thoughts returned to the present when I noticed Infiniti's eyes were wide with excitement. I cringed, afraid of the crazy idea that must've popped in her head.

"Guess what!"

"What?" I answered, eyeing her suspiciously.

"My mom told me last night that after our ski trip she's going on a business trip! You know what that means! Par-tay!" She blasted some music. "It's going to be kick ass!" She opened her laptop and started creating a flyer.

Would my parents find a way to remove my mark by then? Maybe Tavion would find me first and kill me. Or maybe he'd come and kill everyone at the party. There were too many unknown dangers in my life, but one thing was certain. No way could I go to that party.

I hollered over the music, "You're not gonna like this, but I'm not so sure it's a good idea for me to go."

She stopped typing and gave me an open-mouthed look. "What? You're kidding, right?"

"No. I just… you know… it's not my thing. And after the amnesia and the concussion—"

"Hold it right there! I'm putting my foot down!" She stood, raised her petite leg, and slammed her tiny foot on the floor. "You. Are. Going. It'll be good for you. Plus, Trent will be there. Dominique, I've seen the way he looks at you. And when you were out with that concussion, he was so worried. He asked me about you and how you were doing at least a thousand times a day."

I thought of laying with Trent on his bed, and the way Farrell had popped in my head. What did it mean? What had happened between us in our past lives? There had to have been something. Why else would he be so strong a presence in my mind?

Leave the past in the past, I said to myself. Concentrate on the present. Get through this alive and maybe I could be normal and date a normal guy like Trent.

"All right, I'll come. But only for a little while."

She put her arms around me and gave me a hug before returning to her laptop. "This will be good for you, Dominique. I know it."

I stayed at Infiniti's until dark. We had a good time laughing and chatting about everything, especially the party. She even told me that Veronica and Billy had gotten so serious she hardly saw Veronica anymore, which, in my opinion, was a good thing. But of course, I didn't say that.

At around nine or so, I left. It was nice getting away from my problems. But now, as I walked home in the cold, fresh worry set in. My fingers twisted my hair. My mind wondered about what else might be in store for me.

"Dominique?"

I jumped out of my skin and almost called out for Farrell when I saw Jan on the other side of the street. Her dark coat blended in with the night. She came out halfway into the street, and I did the same. "I've got some hot water on the stove," she said cautiously. "Care to come in for some tea?"

I tried to think of a way to say no, but I was never good at making excuses. "Um, well—"

She moved closer to me. "I don't get many visitors, other than your friend Infiniti, and I'd hate to waste some delicious tea I recently purchased. It'll warm you up."

Great, she was laying the guilt on me. How could I say no? And seriously, how dangerous could she be with Farrell down street and my shield reinforced?

"Okay. But I can't be long."

"Good," she said. She waved me over and I followed her into the house and to the kitchen table. "Have a seat, my dear. I'll check the water."

"Thank you, Jan."

I glanced around the kitchen while she busied herself at the stove. The strong vanilla scent from my first visit still filled the air. I searched for a candle, but couldn't find one. My eyes settled on the glass chandelier over her table. Several interesting objects hung from it: a spoon, a fork, some glass beads, ornaments, and several unusual pieces of metal. There was even a white feather. I eyed it, and shuddered. It looked exactly like the feather from my vision, the one I had in my hand that fell to the ground.

I almost scooted away from the table, ready to leave, when Jan returned with crackers.

"So, Dominique, do you have plans for the upcoming winter break?"

"Well—" I concentrated on her face, intentionally avoiding the feather. "No, not really." I folded and unfolded my hands on my lap under the table. "Do you?"

"Yes, I'll be visiting my hometown in Arizona." She motioned toward the crackers. "I wish I had more food to offer, but I haven't been to the store in days."

"This is perfect, thank you." I grabbed a cracker even though my stomach had tied in knots. Stale flakes filled my mouth, and I swallowed them down with a big gulp.

The teapot started to whistle. Jan took the pot off the stove and poured the hot water into two dainty rose-colored teacups. She brought them over to the table along with an array of tea bags. I picked one, and so did she. Silence hovered over us while we dunked our bags. Trying to avoid the chandelier, I studied her hands. I couldn't help but notice the contrast between them and the teacups. The teacups were small and dainty while her hands were big and strong.

"Dominique, do you want to know how I ended up here in Houston?"

Warm, minty tea slid down my throat, and calmed me a little. "Sure," I said, my hands relaxing a bit on my lap.

"Before moving here, I lived in a small town:

93

Oracle, Arizona. I was born and raised there. I loved everything about it—the rustic atmosphere, the serenity, the calmness." She paused, no doubt recalling images of her hometown. "I worked as an artist, doing stitchery for the locals. I didn't make much, but I enjoyed my work. Plus, the flexibility allowed me to pursue other interests."

Her deep, vibrating voice held me captive. "One day, about a year ago, and right before I moved here to Houston, I spotted a small elementary school near my neighborhood. I must've driven by that school hundreds of times, but I hadn't noticed it before. But something about the school spoke to me that day, so I decided to stop and go in. I introduced myself to the school administrator and asked if I could volunteer to read to the younger grades. They were happy to have me, and even scheduled me to come back and read the next day to the kindergarten class. I don't have any children of my own, and so I thought that maybe my maternal instincts were leading me there... and I always follow my instincts."

She stopped for a moment to sip her tea. My eyes darted up to the feather for a second, to see if it was still there, and it was. My mind started coming up with excuses for why I had to leave, but nothing came out.

"The next day, I went to the school as assigned. The teachers were ready for me and even picked out the books for me to read. I couldn't tell you what the books were about, but I can tell you about the child I met that day.

"She was small for her age and stayed at the

back of the room, almost separated from her classmates. When I walked in, her gaze glued on me, and remained fixed on me my entire visit. She wore a simple, yet elegant, white dress, almost like an Easter dress. Her long, white hair flowed down to her back, and her green eyes sparkled bright. She had pale skin, and I thought she might be sick."

Jan took another sip. "After reading a few books, I went to her and introduced myself. She told me her name was Abigail. I can almost hear her now. Her voice sounded steady and clear, not quite matching her somewhat frail exterior. It was strange, yet at the same time, so natural. It's hard to explain."

Jan's eyes darted up for a moment and lingered there, as if lost in her memory of that day. I followed her line of sight and saw that her eyes had landed on the feather. She swiftly brought her attention back to me, and my body tensed.

"We sat there, Abigail and I, surrounded by silence for a while, when she said the strangest thing. She asked me why I didn't live in Houston, Texas. Her question surprised me. After a moment, I told her I didn't know I was supposed to be in Houston. Do you know what she said then?"

I shook my head, completely engrossed by her story, words escaping my lips.

"She said, 'you are.'" Jan stopped and stared at me for a moment. "We sat in silence again, and then the young girl glanced over my shoulder as if looking at someone. I turned to see who it was, but didn't see anyone. When I turned back around, Abigail was gone. I figured she had gone to the restroom, but I couldn't wait for her return since I had another appointment that day. And so I left. But her words stayed with me all day — and her face."

Again, Jan stopped to sip her tea. Again, I followed.

"I never wanted to move, never conceived of leaving Oracle, but Abigail's words haunted me for days, compelling me to listen. Now, I'm here."

My stomach tightened while I clasped my hands together again. Jan took another sip of her tea, but I couldn't. Instead, I stared at my cup, trying to figure out what to say. I cleared my throat. "What happened to Abigail?" A part of me wanted to know, but another part of me was afraid to know.

"I went back to the school the next week, back to the kindergarten class to read again. I searched for Abigail, but didn't see her anywhere. After I did my readings, I asked the teacher about Abigail, curious about her whereabouts. The teacher explained to me that there was no child named Abigail in the class. In fact, she said there wasn't a child named Abigail in the entire school."

I dropped my cup. It shattered on the floor. Shards of the floral pattern scattered everywhere.

"Oh, dear, I've gone and frightened you," Jan said.

I bent down to clean my mess, my hands shaking from fear. "No, it's fine. You're story just surprised me is all."

Jan went to the kitchen sink, grabbed a wet cloth, and knelt beside me. Tension grew around us while we worked to mop up the liquid and pick up the glass. I worked as fast as I could so I could hurry and get out of there.

"Dominique, I'm here to help you." She extended her hand and squeezed my arm with a reassuring grip. "Don't be scared."

"I'm not scared," I lied. "I just don't know why you wanted to tell me that story." I tugged my arm from her grasp.

"It's you, Dominique. You're the reason I moved to Houston. I'm sure of it."

My breathing stilled, my heart almost came to a complete stop. I looked at the chandelier, checking for the feather, but it was gone.

Farrell, I need you!

A loud pounding from the front door jarred the house. "Open up! Dominique? Are you in there?"

"Seems there's someone here for you," Jan said in a perfectly calm voice. "Yes!" she called out. "We're coming!"

Farrell… he heard me and he came.

Jan opened the door and we were met with Farrell's raised fist about to slam against the door again. His face tensed, his brow furrowed. He came to my side and placed his hand on my shoulder.

He half whispered to me, "You okay?"

"Yeah," I whispered back, then cleared my throat. "This is Jan Kelly. We were having tea." My voice sounded shaky, even though I tried my best to keep it steady.

"I'm Farrell Walker." Farrell extended his hand for a shake.

Although the burn on his arm from Tavion

had almost completely healed, the lighting from above landed in such a way that the white streaks stood out. Jan eyed them. She hesitantly reached out, almost afraid to touch him. He noticed her reluctance and let his hand fall down.

"I'm here to get Dominique," he said.

The quiet room filled with the booming gong of a clock. I grabbed Farrell's arm, scared and startled. And then I saw, from where we stood by the front door, the picture of the little girl that hung in the living room. The long white hair, white dress, and green eyes—it was Abigail. I knew it. And she was staring right at me.

Jan spoke. "You better get along then. It was nice to meet you, Farrell. And thank you for the company, Dominique."

Jan kept the door open and watched while Farrell and I walked to the sidewalk. "Dominique, can you come back here for a moment?"

I stopped dead in my tracks. Should I go back? Or keep walking? Farrell frowned and shook his head ever so slightly. "Don't," he warned.

He didn't want me to go back, but something in Jan's voice compelled me. "Hold on," I whispered to him.

Instead of going back to the front door, I stopped midway. The worry lines around Jan's face deepened, or maybe it was the lighting from the porch.

"Dominique, if you need someone to talk to, I'm here for you."

Everything about Jan chilled me to the bone. The soul reading, the story of Abigail, the way she thought she had moved here because of me, the feather hanging from her chandelier that had disappeared. But what if she was right? What if she could help me?

CHAPTER *Eleven*

FARRELL SHOVED HIS HANDS IN his pockets and kept quiet during our walk home. I could tell he wanted to say something, but I didn't give him the chance, walking at a quick pace with my arms crossed.

When we got home, I went straight for my room, turned on all my lights, and buried myself under my covers. Everything Jan had told me stayed with me, her story about Abigail so vivid in my head I feared the girl would appear in my room, like a ghost. I told myself that if she did materialize, I'd call for Farrell and he'd come.

Farrell—my personal protector who'd been with me for lifetimes—if only he remembered what had happened in each life, maybe we'd have a chance this time.

At just past midnight, and nowhere close to sleep, I decided to pay him a visit After all, he had checked on me that one night, why not check on him?

I tiptoed down the hall, and it seemed like

forever before I got to his door. I turned the knob and gave it a small push, and then another and another, until it opened all the way. When my eyes adjusted to the darkness, I saw Farrell in bed, twisting from side to side. Fear tightened my chest. I hesitated to get closer, but what if he needed me? Six more steps and I was at his bedside, about to touch his shoulder, when he called out my name. I sucked in my breath, wondering if I should wake him, when he sat up and grabbed my arm. He jerked my body close. Our eyes locked, but it was as if he didn't see me, as if he didn't know who I was.

"Farrell, wake up. It's me, Dominique."

His eyes were wild, his breathing heavy and warm on my cool cheek.

"Farrell, it's me!"

He blinked a few times before recognizing me. He released my arm. "Dominique? What are you doing here? Are you okay?"

"Yes, I'm fine. Are *you* okay?"

He ran his fingers through his hair. "I'm good. I didn't mean to startle you."

His face relaxed, and I took that as an invitation to stay. I sat on the edge of the bed. "What were you dreaming about?"

"Nothing," he said.

So he had secrets, too. An uncomfortable silence filled the room. My hand shot up to my hair.

"You should really do something about that nervous habit," he added.

I stopped mid-twist and brought my hand down. "I know. It's a dead giveaway, isn't it?"

He smiled. "Yes, it is."

I started to get cold sitting there in my boxers and T- shirt, and I started shivering. Farrell sat up and wrapped his comforter around my shoulders, exposing his perfectly sculpted chest.

"It's supposed to be in the teens tonight, a record for Houston," he said. "If the weather holds, it might even snow in a few days."

A low in the teens for December was cold, even by Michigan standards. "How do you know so much about the weather?" I joked.

"I can just tell," he said. "But what I can't tell is what happened at Jan's that led you to call out for me."

He didn't know what I was doing unless he was with me. That was good to know, and something I had wondered He sat closer to me. "Are you going to tell me what happened over there?"

I didn't know why I resisted telling Farrell and my parents everything, but I did. I needed to keep some things for myself. "It was nothing. Dropped my cup, that's all."

His silence told me he didn't believe my answer, so I had to give him something. "I didn't have a vision, if that's what you're wondering. In fact, the last one I had was when I played the Ouija board."

"Good, and now that your shield has been reinforced you shouldn't see that red desert again. And if you do, then we'll know you're exposed." He took my hand. "If that happens, I'll be there for you. No matter what."

SUNDAY, A DAY OF REST. And for me, a day of reflection. Everything was happening so fast I needed to organize the events in my head. I had moved to Houston after Thanksgiving. Two weeks later, I had discovered I was living my final life, life number nine. I had seen visions of a red desert where I had died in each of my prior lives. My parents revealed they were ancient energy beings known as Transhumans, and that they were Pures protecting me from the evil Tainted. The hottest guy ever lived under my roof, a Pure known as a walker assigned to protect me. And then there was Trent from school, also hot, and very normal. Infiniti planned a party over winter break, while I planned to stay alive. Or at least, stay out of the red desert.

Mom and Dad had wanted to pull me out of school, but I wouldn't let them. Going to school was my path to college, and college was my way back home to Elk Rapids. I couldn't let them take that normalcy away from me. After giving it some thought, Mom and Dad agreed to do things, as much as possible, my way. I was shocked, but relieved.

And so I went back to school on Monday. It was easy enough to get up in the morning, especially since I had stayed up practically all night. I grabbed my favorite old jeans, pulled on a long-sleeved undershirt, and layered that with a red sweater. A car muffler rumbled from outside. Recognizing the sound right away, I peeked through my blinds and saw Trent's car.

The doorbell rang. "Dominique," Dad called out a few seconds later. "You have a visitor."

"I'll be down in a minute."

I tossed my hair up in a half bun, washed my face, brushed my teeth, and slipped my feet into my favorite brown boots. When I got downstairs, I found Trent in the foyer, holding a brown paper lunch sack.

"Good morning, beautiful," he said.

"Good morning," I said, feeling my cheeks flush.

He held up the bag. "Breakfast tacos! My grandmother wanted me to bring them. Hope that's okay."

"That's great, thank you." I took the bag, and it warmed my hands. "Ooh, nice and fresh." I gave a whiff and my mouth watered. "They smell delicious."

"Yep, I think you're gonna like them," he said. Before I could invite him in, he opened the door to leave. "I gotta go. See you at school?"

"Yeah, see you there." It bummed me out that he didn't want to stay, but I couldn't blame him. I hadn't exactly responded to his advances, especially when we were on his bed.

I took the tacos and went to the kitchen. Dad sat at the table pouring over some notes. He sipped his usual caramel-flavored coffee before eyeing me and the sack in my hand.

"These are breakfast tacos from my friend's grandmother." I put the tacos on the table and got some plates.

The house was silent save for the crackling from the fireplace. Dad put his papers down and gave me his full attention. "Dominique, I'm sorry about everything that's happening."

I had always been daddy's girl. Dad and I used to fish together every weekend at Elk Lake and work on puzzles almost every night. Things changed when I was about twelve. He started working more and more until I hardly saw him. I remembered being hurt and angry about his absence. Now it all made sense.

"It's okay, Dad."

Mom and Farrell walked in and noticed the somber mood right away. I could see it on their faces. A loud honking broke the depressing vibe. Infiniti — time for school.

She cranked the heater and the music, and hollered over the songs while we drove to school. From the corner of my eye, I could see Farrell in the back seat, staring out the window. He was the main one who didn't want me going to school, saying it wasn't safe. I actually agreed, but would never let them know. I was willing to risk a lot to feel normal, even if only for a little while.

"Can you guys freakin' believe we only have one more week of school left before the holidays?" Infiniti asked, driving with one hand while putting on mascara with the other. "I'm soooo ready for a break."

Even while putting on her makeup, she managed to get us safely into the parking lot and in our regular spot. Farrell hopped out of the car and opened my door.

"Whoa, what's this?" Infiniti asked, all smiles. "Are you guys…?" She pointed back and forth between us.

"We're dating," Farrell said. "Dominique didn't tell you?"

I spun around and faced him. Why would he say such a thing? I narrowed my eyes and glared at him because I knew exactly why. He needed to stay close to protect me, and this was his solution. Not mine.

"We are not dating," I said, more to him and less to Infiniti.

Infiniti laughed and started walking ahead of us. "It's cool. You guys actually look really good together. Now come on, lovebirds. It's freezing."

Arms crossed, and one step ahead of Farrell, I walked to the building. What was he doing? And what about Trent? I wanted to turn around and go back home. Or maybe that was Farrell's plan, his way of trying to get me to stay home. Well, it wasn't going to work.

My mind filled with anger all the way to first period. After a minute or so, Trent came in, flashed me a smile, and sat next to me. Ms. Ryken followed and handed me a slip of paper. She still wanted to meet after school to talk about college. *Great.* I crammed the paper in my bag, not sure if I would show or not, when Veronica came strolling up to my desk.

She placed her long red fingernails on my desk. "Congratulations on your new boyfriend. Must be convenient having him right under your roof. Dominique and Farrell. Has a nice ring to it."

My cheeks flushed. What a bitch. She sauntered back to her seat. I glanced at Trent. His smile had erased, his bright eyes dimmed. "It's not like that," I said to him.

He turned away. "It's cool. You don't have to explain anything to me."

My heart sank.

I spent the rest of the day doing my best to avoid all human interaction, even though Farrell did remain close, making it look like we were together. At the final bell, Infiniti met me at my locker. She approached with caution.

"I heard about what Veronica said in first period."

"Oh, yeah?" I threw my books in my locker. "And how exactly did she even hear that rumor about me and Farrell, huh?"

"Well, I kind of mentioned it to Billy when I saw him in the hall, but I had no idea he'd text Veronica so fast, and no idea that she'd be all bitchy like that. I swear."

Veronica's red nails on my desk and the look on Trent's face played over and over in my head as I shoved papers into my backpack. I pushed my frustration aside, deciding I needed her intel. "Did Trent say anything to you about it?"

She bit her bottom lip. "Well, he found me at lunch. Asked me if it was true."

My hands trembled. "What did you say?"

"I told him I didn't know, because, well, I don't know!"

My life couldn't get any worse. I slammed my locker shut and started walking away from Infiniti. "I gotta go see Ms. Ryken."

"Um, okay," she said with a fake cheerful voice. "I'll be in the library. Come get me when you're finished."

I walked down the hall and back to Ms. Ryken's classroom. When I entered, I glanced at Trent's empty desk. He had to hate me. And I couldn't blame him. Even I would hate me.

"Hello there, Miss Wells," Ms. Ryken said. I took the seat closest to her desk and tried my best to put on a friendly face. "Are you ready to discuss your future?"

Future? I choked up because I didn't know if I had a future. I clasped my shaky hands together on my lap and forced myself to calm down.

"Dominique, are you okay?" She backed away from her desk and sat next to me, offering me a tissue box.

I couldn't say anything. If I did, I'd lose it. Instead, I shook my head, letting her know I was definitely not okay. Ms. Ryken sat silent for a while, giving me some time to pull it together.

"The idea of leaving high school and going to college can be tough for some. You'll be leaving behind family and friends, but gaining so much more: new friends, tremendous knowledge, a sense of independence."

Again, I said nothing because she had no idea why I was so upset. It wasn't college at all, it was me. My life. My identity. Dying in a red desert. Wanting to be a normal girl with a normal guy.

"Dominique, would you prefer to meet later? Maybe after the break?"

"Sure," I managed to choke out. "Later sounds good." Little did she know I'd probably be dead after the holidays.

"And, Miss Wells, I have something I think you might need." She went to her desk, opened her top drawer, and pulled out a long, beautiful white feather. I gasped, my thoughts taking me to the white feather I had seen in my vision and later at Jan's.

"A white feather," I mumbled.

"It's a funny story," she said. "I like to take long walks in the wooded area by my house. One day, I got a little lost and started to worry, especially since the day had started to turn to night. I couldn't tell which path to follow, but then I spotted this feather. When I picked it up, calmness came over me, and I immediately knew where to go. It was like the feather pointed me in the right direction."

She held the feather out to me. "Here, take it."

"Ms. Ryken, I can't."

She extended the feather closer to me. "Of course you can."

When I touched the feather, a tingle of energy connected at my fingertips. I flinched and closed my eyes, waiting for heat and dust to fill my senses, but it never came. Instead, a warm and soft breeze caressed my face, followed by the smell of sand. I opened my eyes to find myself standing on the shore of Elk Rapids beach.

The blue water filled with tiny ripples from the gentle wind. Way out in the horizon the water blended in with the cloudless sky. But how could I be here? How was it possible?

"You need to think of this place when you're scared."

I spun around and saw Farrell sitting on a nearby cluster of rocks. "You're comfortable here."

Home, where I longed to be. Of course I wasn't afraid here. I sat beside him and scooped up the sand with both hands, letting it sift through my fingers. "This isn't real," I said. I glanced around and didn't see anyone else. On a day like this, the beach would've been crowded.

"Yes and no. Yes, it's real, but only to us. We're the only ones occupying this space right now." His eyes glued on mine and his head tilted to the side as if waiting for me to remember something.

"I'm afraid of dying," I said. "Not so much the death part, but the not living part." I scooped up another handful of sand and held it tight, the gritty granules hardening into a ball. "There's so much I still want to do."

"I know," he said. "But there's always hope. The end is not yet written." He looked up and I followed his gaze. The deep, blue sky had filled with stars — millions of them, the day suddenly turning to night. He stood and brushed off his jeans. "You ready to go back?"

No, I wasn't. Not at all. This was home, a place I longed to be.

He held out his hand. "It's time to go."

My gaze went back to the stars that now streaked across the heavens. The beauty of the night took my breath away. Farrell came by my side. I wrapped my fingers around his. In a flash, I was back in Ms. Ryken's room, the feather resting in the hand Farrell had just grasped.

"Dominique, are you okay?"

"I'm—" My eyes darted around, making sure I was really back in the classroom. "Fine." I blinked a few more times, but nothing happened. I looked back at the feather.

Ms. Ryken followed my gaze. "You need this more than me." She wrapped my fingers around it. "Just remember to follow the path."

"The path…" I repeated.

"Yes," she said. "Everyone has a destiny to fulfill. I call it the path. Sometimes the path is unknown to us— sometimes the path changes. Still, other times, we must forge our path. Either way, nothing happens until we are ready. Understand?"

"Yes, I think I understand." Up until now, things were happening to me. It was like I had no control over my destiny. But forging a path meant taking deliberate steps, calculated action. I didn't know what or how, but I was definitely ready to move forward and create my own path; ready to do things my way.

CHAPTER Twelve

I PLACED THE FEATHER IN a book, thanked Ms. Ryken for her time, and got out of there. I needed to find Farrell. I rushed to the side exit of the school where we always parked, and saw him waiting outside the glass doors. I burst through them, put my stuff on the ground, and got in his face. He shoved his hands in his pockets and waited for me to speak. The smell of sand still lingered around me.

"Were we really there? At the beach?"

"Yes. We were."

"How? I don't get it." I stared at my hands. I could still feel the sand sifting through them.

"Dominique, you need to trust us, and yourself. It's the only way." He ran his fingers through his hair. "You've heard of the saying there's strength in numbers, right? Well, we're stronger when we're together."

"But I don't even know you," I whispered.

Hurt flashed across his eyes, I could tell, but why? There was nothing between us. If anything, the one I wanted was Trent. But now that Farrell had announced we were dating, that would be impossible.

"Listen, I know you're trying to help, but we're not a couple," I said. "Got it?"

"Got it."

My mind raced with everything Ms. Ryken had said about destiny and finding your path when ready. Well, I was ready. "From now on we do things my way, okay?"

He nodded.

That was it? A simple nod? He didn't have any objections?

"There you are!" Infiniti approached with an exasperated look on her face, then slowed her approach, realizing she was barging in on a serious conversation. "You guys having a little alone time?" she asked, raising her eyebrows up. "Need me to leave?"

"No," I declared. "We weren't."

Infiniti drove home with the radio blaring. I was grateful for the music because I didn't want to talk. How could I? I kept thinking of the feather Ms. Ryken had given me and the beach I had visited with Farrell. In fact, my thoughts were so deep I didn't even feel the car stop in front of my house.

Infiniti snapped her fingers in front of my face. "You cool?"

"Yeah, I'm cool."

Farrell and I got out of the car and made our way to the door. When we got there, Jan popped into mind. The feather Ms. Ryken had given me looked exactly like the one at Jan's. That was it.

The first step on my new path was to Jan's.

Once inside, I dumped my stuff on the dining room table. "I'm going to Jan's."

Farrell's eyes narrowed. "Not without me."

"If something happens and I call for you, you'll show up. So technically, I don't need you with me."

He flinched, and I immediately regretted being so cold. "I'll be fine. And I won't be long."

The frigid air chilled my face and a couple of snow flurries floated by as I walked to Jan's. Snow, in Houston of all places like Farrell had said. I held my hand out and watched tiny snowflakes land on my glove. Nothing like back home, but close enough.

When I got to Jan's, I paced the sidewalk for a while, rehearsing what I would say to her. I didn't have to think about it too long because her front door opened.

"Dominique," she said. "What a pleasant surprise. I was coming out to admire our rare winter snow. How are you, dear?"

"I'm good, thanks. I was coming to pay you a visit. I, uh, need your help."

She froze in place for a minute, stared at me, and then closed her eyes. "It is time," she whispered. "Come inside, dear."

I followed her to the kitchen and sat at the table—the scenario familiar now. Vanilla oozed in the air, the glass chandelier sparkled with odd and unusual decorations, and Jan prepared tea. The one difference? The white feather hanging from the fixture was still gone. I wondered what had happened to it.

Jan set the teacups on the table and sat across from me.

"Jan, the last time we spoke you said you were here for me. Well, I'm in trouble. There is something going on with me that I don't understand. Please, can you help me?"

Jan never blinked. Her eyes never left mine. I waited for a response, but she gave none. It was like she had lost her ability to speak. She reached out and grasped my wrist. "Yes."

That was it; that was all I needed to hear. Finally, I was not alone.

"In order for me to help you, I must know everything."

And so I told Jan everything that had happened to me since moving here. She took it all in without blinking an eye. When I finished, a wave of relief washed over me.

She stared at me for a moment. "May I see the back of your neck?"

"Sure." I gathered my hair over to one side of my neck, pulled my collar down, and turned to show her my birthmark.

"It's an interesting mark," she said. "It almost looks like —" She paused before placing her finger on the spot. "Like someone touched you with a burning fingertip."

I swallowed hard. "I guess you could describe it like that."

She moved away from me and closed her eyes, rubbing her creased temples in a circular motion. There had to be something she could do to help me. There just had to be. She started mumbling to herself, repeating some of what I had told her.

"Marked by evil, last life, shielded, no aura, no memory, energy beings." Her eyes snapped open. "I've got it. Wait here a moment."

She left the room and returned with a small red velvet bag. She opened it and brought out several different shaped and colored crystals: pink, gold, blue, clear, green, purple, and black. Some were jagged and long, others smooth and small. They were beautiful and sparkly.

She touched each one. "Crystals have been around since the dawn of civilization. They're powerful because they contain pure energy." She placed them in front of me. "I guess you could say that they too are energy beings."

"What? These hard stones? Like Mom, Dad, and Farrell?" I tried to wrap my brain around that concept, but had a hard time. She could tell I was skeptical.

"Dominique, everything in the universe emits energy, from the smallest blade of glass to the largest mountain. What crystals do is help you hone your energy, understand it, and even use it to your advantage. Understand?"

I wanted to touch the crystals, especially the darkest one. "Yes, I think so."

"Good. Now touch the one that's calling you." My hand went for the black stone. It was the size and shape of a quarter, but thicker. My fingers rubbed the smooth surface and a hint of vibration pulsed in my palm. I brought it close and eyed it carefully. It wasn't black at all, but dark green with flecks of red and gold.

"That is bloodstone, the stone of courage," Jan explained. "It is said that the power of that stone

116

overcomes enemies. Soldiers often carried it in battle."

I remembered Farrell's words when he and my parents had explained who I was. The final battle for the marked one is upon us. My fingers wrapped around the stone. I needed its energy and strength, needed to build my courage. I held it for a while, letting its power seep into me.

Jan held out her hand. "Here, let me see if I can glean anything from your interaction with the stone."

When I gave it to her, she closed her eyes. The room darkened. The vanilla in the air intensified. Her body twitched, her face grimaced, and she shook her head back and forth. "No!" she called out, dropping the stone on the table.

I freaked and backed away from the table, expecting the stone to explode or something.

Jan looked at me with fear-filled eyes. "Dominique, remind me, when is your birthday?"

That's right. My eighteenth birthday was coming up. "January second."

"Oh dear," she said. She closed her eyes, her mouth moving in silence as she did the math in her head. "Two weeks," she muttered.

My pulse quickened. My hands shook. "What is it?"

"Your battle will occur before your eighteenth birthday. It always has, I saw it."

"My death?"

Jan squeezed my hand so tight that my fingertips turned puffy and red. "Yes," she said. "Your death."

My eyes landed on the stone of courage,

carried by soldiers who went into battle. I had touched its energy, but would it stay with me?

"I'm leaving for a trip tomorrow back to my home town, back to Oracle," Jan said. "I'll see what I can find out while I'm there." She released my hand. "While I'm gone, you need to do what you can here on your end. You must discover the truth in what your parents seek."

The truth? They had told me they were searching for a way to remove my mark. Obviously, there was more to it than that.

"Oh, and one more thing," Jan said, her lip quivering. "The one hunting you has help. They search for you now. I felt it."

Panic filled me. My eyes went to the dark stone again.

Please, let me win this time.

CHAPTER Thirteen

I DIDN'T TELL MY PARENTS or Farrell about what Jan had said about dying before my eighteenth birthday, or about Tavion having help tracking me, because I didn't know if it was true. And if it was, then they probably already knew. Besides, Mom and Dad spent most of their time searching for a way to remove my mark. Why worry them more than they already were?

My stomach stayed in a permanent knot. Farrell kept encouraging me to eat, but I rarely did. A granola bar here and there was all I could take. But the worst thing for me was the evenings. At night, thoughts of death haunted me. And the silence, it smothered me tight. Some nights I thought of asking Farrell to sleep in my room. He could camp out on the floor or the oversized chair in the corner of my room. But every time I came close to asking him, I thought of Trent.

I hated that Trent thought Farrell and I were dating, hated that he probably thought he was second best, because he wasn't. Sadly, he would never know because what was the point? I was going to die soon anyway.

The last day of school before the break came and went, and I had a hard time believing Christmas was a week away. Snow blanketed the north, but here in Houston the days shifted from freezing to sunny and warm, in the high seventies during the day and forties at night. Like the changing weather, I needed to change. Time was running out for me, and I was ready to fight for survival.

One night, when my parents were gone and Farrell was asleep, I crept into my dad's study. Jan's words echoed in my mind with each step… *You must discover the truth in what your parents seek.* Maps and documents stacked high on the desk. I wasn't sure where to start when again I thought of Jan's words when she showed me the stones… *Touch the one that's calling you.* I closed my eyes and calmed my nerves. When I opened my eyes, I saw Abigail! Her white-laced dress hung down to her feet. Her long, white hair combed behind her ears. She held a small, brown book. I shut my eyes, hoping she'd go away, when a hand touched my arm. A scream shot out of me.

"Dominique!" It was Farrell, standing in front of me, his hand on me. "Are you okay?"

"Did… did… you see her?" I spun around, looking for Abigail.

He followed my gaze around the room. "Who?"

Abigail had disappeared, but the book she held was on the floor. I knelt down to pick it up. The leather cover crinkled under my fingertips.

The pages were thick and yellowed, and a gold embossed feather pattern lined the edges. *Feathers, another sign.*

Farrell zeroed in on the book. "What's that?"

My fingers touched the crackled pages. They were water-damaged. Small, black, cursive writing bled out on almost every page. "I don't know. It was on the floor when I walked in." I kept the part about Abigail to myself. I didn't want Farrell knowing I had started seeing ghosts. I wasn't sure he'd believe me.

I examined the first page, trying to make out the words. "There's a name and a date." Peering closer I said, "Julian Huxley. Transhumanism. 1930."

Farrell took the book. "Julian Huxley? 1930?" He flipped through the pages. "We need to tell your parents, right away."

My heartbeat sped up. "Why? Who's Julian Huxley?"

"Julian Huxley is a famous scientist. He was the first professor of biology at the Rice Institute, now known as Rice University. He coined the term transhumanism in a paper he wrote in 1956. He's the reason your parents moved here. They think his studies can help find a way to remove your mark." He glanced down at the book. "This journal, written twenty-seven years before his paper, could be the answer."

"Transhumanism?" I sat in front of my dad's laptop and searched the term. The screen filled with resources. I read two aloud. "Reader's Digest Great Encyclopedia, 1966. Transhumanism is defined as surpassing, transcending, beyond.

Webster's New Universal Dictionary, 1983. Transhuman is defined as superhuman, and transhumanize is defined as to elevate or transform to something beyond what is human."

Stunned, I thought of the things Farrell could do. Thought of how my parents explained what it meant to be a Transhuman, an energy being like humans, but with more brain neurons.

"This Julian Huxley is talking about you guys, isn't he?"

Farrell studied me before answering. "Yes, he is."

I took the book from Farrell and studied the first page more carefully. My eyes began to make out the water stained ink, and I read the first few sentences out loud. "Cosmic self-awareness is man understanding his past history and possible future. This type of awareness has been realized elsewhere too, I imagine, on the planets of other stars. But here, on our planet, it has never happened before. Until now."

My mind raced. *Other planets*? Were Farrell and my parents aliens? "Farrell, he mentions other planets."

"Yes, he does, and in that one detail Mr. Huxley is wrong. Transhumans are not from other planets. We're from Earth, and we've existed long before humans. Some refer to us as the first people, others as angels. Somewhere in the middle lies the truth."

Humans with superpowers, the stuff movies are made of. How could it be? And then I thought of Julian Huxley. How did he even come up with his ideas?

"Farrell, how did this guy even know about Transhumans?"

"He found one of us. He studied her in an effort to understand us. We know she later died, but we don't know how. She was a young girl named Abigail."

My mouth dropped. My skin crawled. "A girl with pale skin and long white hair?"

Farrell tilted his head to the side a little. "Yes, how did you know that?"

Time to confess. "Jan told me about her, and I actually saw her, right here in this room. She was holding the book. I should've told you, but I thought you wouldn't believe me. Anyway, she obviously wanted me to find it."

Farrell paced the room while my mind worked overtime. Abigail was a Transhuman, and now she was trying to help me. Maybe my salvation was in the damaged pages. Since Mom and Dad weren't answering their phones, there was only one thing to do.

"We need to take this to them," I said. "Do you know where they are?"

"They're at Rice studying the writings of Huxley kept in the library."

Several missed calls later, and after a quick change of clothes, we were off.

Farrell drove Mom's car while I used my phone to look up directions to the school, which was quite a distance away — down three major highways and almost to downtown Houston. We turned from Highway 290 onto the 610 Loop. When we merged, the downtown buildings seemed to erupt out of nowhere, looking like its own little sparkling city of skyscrapers. Some buildings even twinkled with Christmas lights.

"Wow," I said.

"It's nice, isn't it," Farrell said.

"Yeah, it's actually pretty amazing. I had no idea."

Travelling to yet another highway, highway 59, I marveled at how pretty downtown was. Finally, we exited the massive freeway and turned down a street that went through a neighborhood. After a few more turns, we drove onto the campus and parked.

Shrubs and trees nestled the school. Beyond the parking lot, a large, perfectly mowed lawn led up to a modern building. The long sand and pink-colored stone structure had a flat roof, save for a tall rectangular middle with a huge archway. Extending on either side of the main arch were smaller arches that formed a walkway. As we got closer, I noticed multiple white columns lining the front. Instead of looking like a college, it looked more like a fortress.

I held the book tight while we hurried through the main archway and into a grassy quadrangle. In the middle was a bronze statue of a man on a chair wearing a robe and holding a book. Farrell pointed to the building on the other side of the monument. "That's the library."

The cool, crisp air carried a hint of dew, but suddenly dry air and heat assaulted me. I stopped and grabbed Farrell's arm, waiting for the red desert to appear, but nothing happened.

"What's wrong?" he asked.

"Something's not right."

Farrell brought me close. We scanned the area, but saw nothing, and that was when I remembered what Jan had said about Tavion and his helpers searching for me. Panic struck me. They had found me; I knew it. I was about to tell Farrell about my suspicion when a crashing thunder shook the sky. A bolt of lightning struck the ground in front of us. I covered my eyes. When I opened them, I saw a guy maybe ten feet away. He was tall and lean, like Farrell, but had short, dark hair.

"A Tracker," Farrell whispered, confirming what I had feared. "When I rush him, you hold that book for dear life and run to the library. I have to stop him."

Without giving me time to respond, Farrell took off. A white light with shades of gold emanated from his body, surrounding him like a shield. I bolted for the library. Looking back, I saw a ball of light gather at Farrell's hands and blast out at the Tracker. Before it could hit, the Tracker disappeared.

Farrell zipped over to me and took my hand. "Come on, we need to get your parents and get out of here."

"What happened?" I panted as we approached the library. "Where did he go?"

"Trackers are not sent to kill. Just to find."

Shit. The Tracker was reporting back to Tavion, Terror exploded inside me. I ran up to the library. The glass doors revealed a small light in a back room. That had to be where my parents were. I was about to bang on the glass when Farrell stopped me. "You'll set the alarm off. Step back."

He closed his eyes, and again the golden light glowed all around him. He put his hand on the glass, and it disappeared. He walked through and motioned for me to follow. As soon as I was on the other side, the glass returned.

My mouth dropped. "How... did you... do that?"

Mom and Dad rushed over to us. "Dominique? Farrell?" Dad asked. "What's going on?"

"Dominique's shield has been compromised. A Tracker has found us," Farrell said quickly. "We must go. Now."

Mom and Dad returned to the back room, grabbed some papers, and turned out the lights. They rejoined Farrell and me by the front door. My heart raced while my eyes focused on the grassy area we had just come from.

Dad eyed Farrell. "Take her out of here."

"Are you sure?" Farrell asked.

"Yes, it's the only way," Dad ordered.

My hands still clutched the book, my pulse raced. "Wait, what? Take me out of here? What about you guys?"

Mom placed her hands on my shoulders. "We'll be right behind you. Now go." She took the book from me. "Now, Walker."

Farrell stood in front of me and held my hands. A memory flashed through my mind. Farrell had done this before; had stood in front of me and held my hands while fear raced through my veins. And now we were doing it again.

"Trust me," he whispered.

I studied his perfectly pointed nose, his green

eyes, and his messy blond hair, thinking he was the most beautiful person I'd ever seen. White radiance seeped out of him and wrap around us like a warm blanket. The glow made me dizzy and lightheaded and completely at peace.

A RAY OF SUNLIGHT WARMED my face. I basked in it for a while, not wanting to open my eyes, when I heard a soft voice. "Dominique, you ready to wake up?"

I opened my eyes to see my mom at my bedside. She held a tray of food. I sat up and made room for her to sit.

"What time is it?" I asked.

The sun shone bright through my window. "It's almost noon." She placed the tray on my lap. "Dad made your favorite omelet—cheese and bacon."

My stomach growled, but clenched tight when I remembered that I had been in front of that library holding Farrell's hands while his energy wrapped around me. "How did I get here?" I pictured Farrell's glowing light taking me over. "Where's Farrell?"

"He's downstairs with your father. He used his energy to bring you here. It's not something we like to do, but it was necessary. Everything's fine now."

My bones ached all over, as if I had competed in a wrestling match the night before. I pushed the tray away.

"Dominique, Farrell had to drain some of

your energy to get you here, but you both made it. We all did." She picked up the plate and held it to me. "Now please, eat."

I took a few bites to make her happy, then found myself finishing the entire plate. I should've been scared as hell that another Tracker would find me, terrified that Tavion was one step closer to my death, but I wasn't. I was too tired. And then I noticed something about Mom, something in her expression that told me she had bad news.

"What is it?' I asked, afraid to hear her answer.

She cleared her voice. "Your father and I have to go out of town. We leave in an hour."

I sat up, almost knocking the food off the bed. "No! You can't!" Tingles of panic flowed through me. "That Tracker found me, Mom! I'm not safe here, nobody is!"

Mom put her hands on my arms. "Dominique, you'll be all right here in this house with Farrell. The Tainted may know you're in Houston, but they still haven't pinpointed your location."

"You don't know that, Mom. For all we know they're outside this house watching me right now, waiting for you guys to leave."

"Dominique, please, trust me. Your father and I reinforced your shield. You're safe, I promise."

My body relaxed a bit. "Really?"

"Yes, really. Plus, we'll only be a few days."

Mom and Dad took Julian Huxley's journal and left, leaving me alone with Farrell. A deep and restless anxiety settled in me. If a Tracker could find me at Rice, it could find me anywhere, even if my parents had reinforced my shield — again.

If only I could do something besides sit around and wait for my death. But what?

I called Jan, but didn't get an answer. Without even thinking, I called Trent, but hung up before the first ring. I hoped my call wouldn't register on his phone. With Infiniti out of town, I had no one else to contact except maybe…Abigail. She had brought me the book after all. But how could I reach out to her? Chills crawled down my spine. The Ouija board, that was how.

CHAPTER *Fourteen*

My mind plotted the different ways to get an Ouija board. Even though Infiniti was in Breckenridge skiing with her mom, I could text her and ask to borrow hers and see if she had an extra key hidden somewhere. Failing that, I could try to break into her house, or I could go to a store and buy one. One way or another, I had to get my hands on one before my parents returned. Only, I had to do it without alerting my protector because I knew he'd be against it.

As if in answer to my prayer, a text from Infiniti came through. Home early. Party tonight at 9! BYOB!

Perfect! I'd go to Infiniti's for a quick appearance, get the board, and make my exit. In and out—Farrell would never know I had left.

At exactly nine, I began my well-planned escape. A hard tug on my window sent a loud screech through my room. My heart pounded as I froze in place, waiting for Farrell to burst into my room, but he didn't. After several long seconds, I opened the window all the way.

Okay, keep going. Crawling through the opening, I stepped out onto the steep roof. Holding my breath, I tiptoed to the corner of the house closest to the backyard fence. I stepped onto the top wooden plank, then jumped down to the grass with a thud. With no sign of Farrell, I let out a long exhale. I had made it.

At Infiniti's, music blared and bodies danced. I said a few hellos here and there, but kept my attention focused on finding Infiniti and asking to borrow her board game. I made my way to the kitchen and found her manning the shot bar.

"Hey, you made it!"

She pushed her long curly hair behind her ears, then filled up two small glasses with liquid that had gold flecks in it. She handed one shot glass to me, and kept the other for herself. She lifted her glass. "To ski trips that don't exactly pan out, and to friends that show up last minute for parties. Cheers!"

I hated shots, but took it for Infiniti, feeling bad that something had happened to cut her trip short. I tossed my head back and downed the liquid that tasted like cough syrup. I shuddered as it slid down my throat, burning a trail right through me.

Infiniti downed her glass and gave a loud YEEHAW. I busted out laughing, realizing I hadn't laughed in a long time, but forced myself to focus on getting the board. I was about to ask for it when she pointed over my shoulder.

"Hey," she hiccupped. "Your boyfriend's here."

I glanced over my shoulder and saw Farrell at the other end of the room, arms crossed, eyes glaring at me. "He's not my boyfriend," I said, clenching my jaw, pissed that he had followed me.

"He'ss hot, dude. What'ss the big deal?" Infiniti slurred.

The big deal was not being able to get away from him, not being able to be with Trent if I wanted, and not being able to live my life. Oh, and dying in a few days.

"It's complicated." I didn't need Farrell to remind me that I needed to get out of there and back to the safety of my house. I took the shot glass out of Infiniti's hand. "Hey, do you still have that Ouija board?"

"Nope, Ver-r-r-onica borrowed it," she stuttered with another drunken hiccup.

My stomach tightened. What? Veronica? Before I could ask why Veronica wanted it, Farrell came up to me. He started to say something when Trent and a handful of soccer players burst into the kitchen. They carried a couple of cases of beer and looked like they had drunk a couple before arriving. Trent wore a baseball cap and dark sunglasses. He acted loud and obnoxious, checking out every girl who walked by. It wasn't him at all, and it made me sick.

Trent spotted Farrell and me right away. I braced myself while he sauntered over to us.

"Farrell, buddy," he said sarcastically. "Can I borrow your ex?"

My mouth dropped, and my heart pounded. I stared at Trent, dumbfounded, but he kept his attention on Farrell. "I mean, she is your ex now, right? At least that's what I heard."

Farrell stared stone-faced at Trent. "You can borrow her only if she wants to be borrowed."

Infiniti's eyes nearly popped out of her head. Trent guzzled his beer, slammed the can on the kitchen counter, and took my hand. "I take your silence as a yes."

He pulled me to the dance floor in the middle of the den. The only light came from a sparkling disco ball in the middle of the room. As if destined to be close to him, the music switched to a slow song. I wanted to walk away, but I froze. Trent took off his sunglasses and cap, tossed them on the couch, placed his arms around my waist, and brought me close. He buried his head in the crook of my neck, and we moved back and forth with the music. His warm breath against my skin and his hard body against mine sent waves of desire through me. He moved his hands down to the small of my back and drew me in closer. He whispered in my ear. "You know you want me."

I pulled away. "Trent, please don't do this."

"You think about me, Dominique. I know it."

"Yes," I whispered, looking down. "I do." And it was true. Even though Farrell kept entering my mind, I often thought of Trent and what it would be like to be with him.

His hands came up to my face. His vulnerable and hurt eyes searched mine. Gradually, the space between us disappeared. He pressed his lips on mine, opening his mouth tenderly. Our kiss was long and slow, but flashes of Farrell filled my mind. And that was when I knew, without a doubt, that Farrell and I had been together in the past.

I pushed him back. "Trent… we… we… can't. It's just… not…" I needed to get out of there—and fast. "I have to go."

I made my way to the front door, shoving bodies out of my path. Without looking back at Trent, or Farrell or Infiniti, I pushed through the crowded foyer, flung open the door, and rushed out into the cool night. My heart raced while I walked home, my lips still tingling from my kiss with Trent, but my heart now filled with Farrell.

Back in the safety of my home, I started to make my way upstairs to my room when I noticed odd shadows coming from the den.

My heart almost stopped. My spine went cold. Was someone in my house? I redirected my steps to investigate, and found Veronica in the middle of my den.

When my eyes met hers, a pain shot through the back of my neck like a knife. I fell to the floor and landed hard on my knees, blinded by the jab. When I opened my eyes, the red landscape flickered before me. It switched back and forth with my den so fast I couldn't make out the scene before me.

After a series of blinks, I spotted the Ouija board on the coffee table. A thick, black mist trickled out of it, encircling Veronica's feet. It drifted up her body. Words failed me as I stared at the phenomenon in complete disbelief, shaking my head from side to side, not wanting to believe my eyes, my vision still shifting at rapid-fire pace. Pain escalated throughout me and kept me rooted in place, my knees pressing hard against the floor.

Veronica's eyes were devoid of emotion. She said in a low voice, "He came to me in whispers during the night and then during the day — whispers I couldn't get out of my head. 'Get the board,' he commanded. 'Help me find her.'"

The vapor trickled up to her chest and shot into her with angry force, her body rigid and stiff until the mist completely absorbed into her. She closed her eyes.

"Veronica?" I whispered through the deafening silence that now filled the room.

Her eyes snapped open. She looked down on me. Her brown pupils had transformed to pitch black.

"Stand," she ordered. It wasn't her voice, but the deep and raspy voice from the red desert. Farrell had called him Tavion, the leader of the Tainted who had been pursuing me in each life. Shivers raced up and down my spine as I reluctantly obeyed her command.

"Tavion?" I thought of my shield. "How?"

A sick grin spread across Veronica's face. "My Tracker led me to you. And this one here, this body that I now occupy, was more than willing to help. I've merely been waiting for you to be alone."

An urgent knock sounded at the front door. "Dominique, it's Trent."

Veronica flicked her fingers, silencing the scream that had nearly escaped my throat. She yanked me by my hair, her cruel touch sending the mark at the back of my neck ablaze with even

135

more pain.

"Dominique, I need to talk to you! Please, let me in!"

Opening my mouth, I tried to force out a warning, but couldn't. He needed to go away. He didn't need to die because of me.

"This is perfect," Tavion said through Veronica's lips. Her evil gaze focused on the door. "When I release your voice, tell him to come in."

Oh, hell no. I shook my head, determined to save Trent. Tavion could do whatever he wanted to me, but now way would I let him hurt anyone else.

A fresh burst of pain plowed through. My body jolted as if I'd been electrocuted. Tears filled my eyes.

"If you tell him to come in, I'll let him live. Refuse, and he's dead." Veronica scraped her tingly fingers over my lips. "Now do it."

My vocal chords opened up, as if a wad of cotton had been yanked from my mouth. "C-come in," I called out in a shaky voice, hoping Trent would detect that I really didn't want him to come in at all.

The door opened and Trent came into the den. Before he had time to take in the scene, the black mist shot out of Veronica's chest and flew into his like an arrow. The blast jerked him off the floor. He let out a howling yell while the vapor disappeared into his chest. He collapsed to the ground with a thump.

"Trent!"

He got up—slowly. He eyed me with a menacing smile, his blue eyes now black as night.

"No," I whispered.

He strode over to Veronica, who seemed to be in a daze. He raised his hand in her direction and closed his eyes. His body gave off a dark glow that gathered into his palm. Then, with a flick, he blasted a spark at her. Her neck snapped with a pop. Her lifeless body slumped to the floor.

"I have no further use for you," Tavion said through Trent with that same deep and raspy voice.

Fear exploded inside me. My thoughts flooded with Farrell. Lightning from outside poured through the windows that lined the room. A crash shook the house. Farrell appeared before me amidst a bolt of crackling light. I wanted to warn him, tell him that Tavion had killed Veronica and taken Trent, but my voice didn't work. Tavion had muffled me again.

"There you are, Walker," Tavion said through Trent's lips. "Still protecting the one you have grown so fond of."

Trent grabbed my arm. He jerked me to him. With every touch, the pain at my neck exploded inside me, my veins throbbing as if fire coursed through them. He pointed his arm at the ground. Black mist curled around his arm and trickled out of his hand until it formed a pool of vapor on the floor, like a swirling hurricane under our feet.

"Release her," Farrell said.

"She belongs to me, Walker."

The pain at my neck throbbed uncontrollably while the churning vapor beneath me grew in size and speed. Weightlessness and nausea came over me, followed by the stench of burnt flesh.

I shut my eyes, thinking my entire body had caught on fire, when suddenly my feet landed on solid ground.

My chest tightened. Heat smothered me and burned my nose. The taste of dirt filtered into my mouth. I opened my eyes to find my house gone, replaced by the red desert. Right in front of me was Jan. She was sprawled out on the ground, her eyes wide, blood trickling out of her mouth.

She was dead.

CHAPTER Fifteen

"YOU'RE BACK WHERE YOU BELONG," Tavion whispered in my ear through Trent's lips. He kissed my earlobe. A burning blast shot through my skin. I shuddered, and tried to yank away, but he tightened his grip.

I stared at Jan, hoping she'd blink, take a breath, but she didn't. Despair filled me because I knew I was next. All of my deaths had led me here, to my final ending. But I wasn't about to let Tavion have me that easy. I raised my arm, rammed my elbow into Trent's gut, and slammed my heel down on his foot. Startled, he loosened his grip. I broke away and raced through the desert, his howling and snarl- filled laughter echoing all around me.

"There's nowhere to run, Marked One!"

He was probably right, but I kept sprinting anyway. Out of nowhere I crashed into something—Trent! He had appeared in my path, his eyes black, his face scowling. He raised his hand in front of my face and formed a fist. Black mist wrapped around his fingers. He opened his hand and sent a stream of vapor at me. It struck me like a head-on collision. I flew through the air and landed flat on my back. Blood filled my mouth as I gasped for air.

Trent's shoes thudded on the ground as he approached for more. I scraped together two handfuls of the gritty, red sand, ready to throw them in his face. He stood over me. He jerked my arm, and pulled me to my feet. A yelp shot out of me and tears blurred my vision.

Wrestling my arms away, I flung the sand at his face. Tavion stopped the particles mid- air with an open hand. When he lowered his hands, the tiny grains dropped to the ground. "Still a fighter," he said with a smile. "Some things never change."

I glanced at Jan's corpse. Her death was on me, but I guess it didn't matter since I was next. But where was my protector? My capture couldn't be that easy, could it? My mind called out to Farrell in desperation. *Farrell! Where are you?*

Crackling streaks of white lightning filled the air and shot across the red sky. "Looks like our friend is here," Tavion said with a smile. "Right on time."

Dazzling lightning filled the sky, streaming to the ground in a gold flash. I shielded my eyes until the brilliance faded. When I brought my hands down, I saw Farrell, and he looked pissed.

Tavion took hold of my arm and brought me closer. He stroked my hair as if I were his pet. He kissed the top of my head.

"Release her," Farrell said to Tavion.

"As you wish," Tavion replied.

He let go of my arm. Afraid to make sudden movement, I inched my way to Farrell's out-stretched hand. When our hands met, he pulled me behind him.

A deep menacing laugh erupted from Trent's lips, a laughter that grew loud and forceful until it morphed into a hideous growl.

Farrell and I backed away. The snarling from Trent filled the air until the deep black mist that had invaded his body blasted out of his chest. Farrell stayed in front of me like a shield as the haze collected and took on the shape of a man.

"Tavion?" I whispered to Farrell.

"Yes, Tavion," he confirmed.

Tavion stood at least a foot taller than Farrell. Dressed in all black, his thin body looked almost skeletal, his cheeks hollow enough to resemble a rotting corpse. Even his short white hair blend-ed in with his face. If death took on a form, this would be it.

Trent's body slumped to the floor. I lurched forward to get him, but Farrell held me back. "Not yet," he whispered. "When I say."

Tavion eyed us. "So Walker, here we are, again. It is good to see you. You look well. And your ward, I like her. It will be a shame to kill her. For the last time."

"I don't think so, Tavion," Farrell said.

Tavion rammed his foot into Trent's gut. I covered my mouth, muffling a gasp.

"What's this? The Marked One likes this hu-man?" He laughed, his vicious gaze landing on me before returning to Farrell. He kicked Trent again. "What do you think of that, Walker?" Tavion lifted his foot and placed it on Trent's head. "What do you think of her affection for this being?"

"Run for Trent when Tavion is out of the way," whispered Farrell, ignoring Tavion's taunts. Before I could agree to the plan, Farrell charged full-on. He knocked Tavion away from Trent. Black and white sparks exploded in the air, as they tumbled to the ground.

I raced to Trent, grabbed his arms, and pulled him to a cluster of rocks big enough to hide behind. Fighting blasts from Farrell and Tavion exploded in the distance as I checked Trent's pulse. It was strong, but his face had lost all color. I stroked his cheek, unable to bear it if I lost him. Veronica had died because of me, and so did Jan. Jan! I spun around, ready to drag her over too, but she had vanished. Or had I imagined her there all along? I had no idea, but I needed to arm myself in case Tavion came back for me.

Desperately searching about, I spotted two jagged stones the size of small hand weights. I grabbed them and held them close, then peered over the rocks. Farrell and Tavion fought while massive flares of white and black surrounded them. I watched in terrified wonder, hoping and praying for Farrell to be okay, when a booming sound sent Farrell soaring through the air. He landed right beside me with a crash. Blood trickled out his mouth and slid down his chin. My heart stopped. I froze in place, waiting for him to move.

He inched himself up on one arm. He wiped

the crimson streak from his mouth while Tavion approached.

"Farrell," I warned. "He's coming."

Farrell staggered to his feet and distanced himself from my protective spot—fists clenched, blood splattered on his shirt. A white glow with sparks of gold gathered around his hands.

"Where am I?" Trent murmured. "What's happening?"

Relief washed over me, but only for an instant because I feared for Farrell. "It's Farrell. He's in trouble."

Tavion picked up his pace. With crackling mist pulsing around his upper body, he threw his arms out. An explosion of black smoke shot at Farrell's chest.

"No!" I yelled.

Farrell swiftly brought his arms together in front of him, his white light forming a shield. The black smoke made contact, but instead of blasting him through, it fizzled out.

"They're fighting with their auras," Trent said in disbelief, now standing by my side. "Their energy source. But... how?"

What? The light and mist that came from Farrell and Tavion, even the Tracker I had seen at Rice, was their auras? That was how they used their energy? Each even had their own color. Farrell's was white with streaks of gold, Tavion's was black, and the Tracker's was gray. Trent had said that his was blue. I searched Trent's body, but couldn't see anything. And me? I didn't even have one. I felt more defenseless than ever.

Farrell glanced back at me and Trent, his

breathing labored, his face bloodied. "Take cover," he said to us.

Tavion growled and shouted, "No more games, Walker!"

Tavion materialized in front of me. He took me by the throat. With a wave of his other hand, he sent Trent flying through the air. He sneered as he formed a black vapor that shot up into the air and then cascaded down on us in shimmery sparks, forming a bubble-like dome around the two of us. Farrell hurled his white light at the barrier, but every assault bounced off. Soon, Trent was at Farrell's side. Together they slammed their fists against the misty dome, but couldn't get through.

Tavion had me.

And Farrell and Trent couldn't do a thing about it.

Tavion's fingers dug into my skin, cutting off my windpipe. I desperately gulped for air, but couldn't get any.

"Now I take your energy source. Like. Always." Tavion licked his lips. He closed his eyes. He brought his other hand to my chest, and plunged it into me.

Searing heat filled my insides, as if he had rammed a burning log straight through me. My fingers clamped around the stones in my hand. The jagged edges cut into my skin and I could feel blood dripped from my fingers. I lifted my arms in an attempt to bash the rocks against Tavion's face, when I lost my strength. My meager weapons dropped to the ground.

I thought of Farrell's words. *You're stron-*

ger than you know, Dominique. I remembered the feather Ms. Ryken had given me that transported me to the beach and what Farrell had said on the shore. *You need to come here when you're scared.*

The image of blue sky, white sand, and calm waters popped into my mind, edging out the fear and terror that had taken over me.

My body slipped to the ground. My knees sank into cool, pebbly sand. A soft breeze flowed through my hair. Farrell stood beside me at the water's edge, staring out at the still lake. He extended his arm and helped me to my feet. I brushed myself off, recalling the terror and pain I had left behind in the red desert. I patted my chest.

"Am I really here?"

"No," Farrell said sadly. "Only your mind is here."

"Farrell, am I — ?" I paused, not wanting to say the words, as if keeping them to myself would change my fate. "Am I dying?"

"Yes." He took my hand. "There's nothing I can do." His calmness filtered into me. And for a minute there, death didn't seem so bad.

My attention turned to a bird in the distance that soared through the cloudless sky. For eight lifetimes now I had died, and this was my last time. The world would never be the same, and it was my fault.

Farrell squeezed my hand. "Remember what I said? The last time we were here?"

Of course I remembered. "You told me the end is not yet written, and to trust myself."

The bird, a white Egret, flew closer. It glid-

145

ed right over us with outstretched wings. A lone, white feather escaped its plumage. The delicate quill drifted back and forth in the sky. Just like the feather from my dreams and the feather Ms. Ryken had given me that I had later seen at Jan's. And then it dawned on me that it was the same colors as Farrell's aura. I extended my hand, reaching out for it. When it touched my palm, it disappeared.

Like flipping a switch, I was back in the desert. Heat exploded inside me. The air in my lungs had almost emptied. Warm, thick blood dripped from my fingers. Farrell and Trent were on the other side of Tavion's dark energy force, and I was still inside, barely alive. Tavion continued to lift me at my throat, squeezing the life out of me.

"Dominique! Fight!" Trent yelled.

More than anything, I wanted to live. I gathered my remaining strength and slapped my bare and bloodied hands against Tavion's face, doing my best to gouge his eyes out. He let out a howling screech that thundered in my ears and shook me to my core. He dropped me, and down came his entrapping energy field.

Trent and Farrell rushed to my side while my eyes stayed glued on Tavion. The blood from my hands had smeared across his face, bubbling and burning his pale skin. I lifted my arms and stared at my bloodied hands. How did I do that?

"We need to get out of here," Farrell rushed out, squeezing my wrist in a death grip. "Trent, hold Dominique, and don't let go." Trent latched on to my other wrist. Farrell closed his eyes. He pointed his free arm at the ground. His aura trickled out of his hand, forming a swirling pool beneath us.

A deep, growling howl filled my ears. Tavion staggered to his feet.

"Farrell! He's getting up!"

Farrell's face strained. Sweat beads formed on his forehead.

"Farrell, hurry, man," Trent urged.

The white vapor started to suck me down into it, but not before Tavion hurled out a blast. Trent draped his body over mine. I braced for impact when weightlessness came over me. My body plummeted before striking solid ground.

When I opened my eyes, I found myself back in my house. In flashes, I saw Trent slumped on the floor facedown, a burn mark streaked across his back. Farrell crouched next to me, his hand still gripping mine. His face was black, blue, and bleeding.

Tavion—his blast must've hit Farrell and Trent before we slipped away.

Ms. Ryken came up from behind Farrell. Her red hair had turned black and flowed down her back. She held a long, white staff. And then I realized I knew her—not from school, but from somewhere else. I remembered the picture of my parents with their college friends, the one of them in front of a cabin. She was in the picture—she was one of their friends.

"Now, Colleen!" Farrell yelled.

She raised her staff and slammed it on the floor. A bright, green light shot out of the top and cascaded down, filling the entire room with a brilliant glow that faded to a pale green.

"We're safe," she said.

She crouched down and checked Trent for a pulse. "Walker, he's almost gone. Quick, bring him back."

Tears filled my eyes. If anything happened to Trent, I'd never forgive myself. "Farrell, please help him."

Farrell went to Trent. He gently eased him over. I gasped when I saw his perfect face charred on one side.

With a soft touch, Farrell placed his fingers on Trent's forehead and closed his eyes. Farrell's white and golden-streaked light trickled out of his hand and absorbed into Trent until Trent's skin glowed from within with Farrell's light. I waited for Trent to move, but nothing happened. Farrell's arms started shaking, his faced strained, and his breathing grew shallow.

Colleen frowned and moved closer to Farrell. "It's not working. You must stop."

Trent was dying, right before my eyes. My breathing stopped while my heart pounded against my chest.

"Stop, Walker!" Colleen called out.

Farrell either didn't hear or didn't want to listen. His light pulsed brighter, and his face turned white from the effort. Colleen pointed her staff at him. She threatened to blast him if he didn't stop, when Trent's body jerked. His mouth opened as he sucked in a gulp of air. Farrell removed his hand from Trent's forehead and fell back. He had done it. He had saved Trent.

Trent's hands went to his chest as he worked to catch his breath. His clothes were singed, his face unrecognizable on one side. I knelt beside him. The tears that had blurred my vision slowly made their way to the surface and slid out onto my face.

"Trent, I'm so sorry."

"He must be healed," Ms. Ryken said to Farrell. "And he must not remember a thing."

"I don't know if I can," Farrell said. "But I'll try."

Trent tried to sit up, but grimaced in pain. He looked at Farrell and Ms. Ryken. "Who the hell are you?" He turned to me. "Dominique, what's going on?"

"I'm so sorry, Trent," I said again. "I didn't mean for any of this to happen."

Farrell touched Trent's forehead. This time Trent passed out. Farrell kept his fingers on Trent. His white mist flowed from his hand and into Trent head. Trent's body trembled, and so did Farrell's. I wanted to go to them, but Ms. Ryken held me back.

"Let the Walker finish," she warned.

Farrell's light grew brighter while Trent's body emanated with a blue glow. *His aura*, I thought to myself. The blue color encircled him, growing darker until Trent vanished. Farrell sat back. "He's back at Infiniti's," he panted. "Healed and wiped. He'll think he passed out from drinking. He won't remember a thing."

My thoughts went to Veronica. She had been killed in this room, but was now gone. Even though I was afraid of the truth, I needed to know what had happened to her. "What about Veronica?"

"Death is beyond our reach," Ms. Ryken explained. "She had already crossed over before I got here. Her passing was made to look like a car accident."

My head grew fuzzy, and I lost my balance. I didn't even realize Farrell took my hands to steady me. I drew them away and studied my blood-stained palms. Deep gashes lined the insides from the jagged rocks.

Farrell reached out. "Here, I can fix that."

"No, leave them," I said. Veronica had died, Trent almost died, and I had no idea what had happened to Jan. The least I could do was keep these stupid cuts.

Farrell looked at my wounds in amazement. "How did you do that?"

"Do what?" Colleen said, coming in closer for inspection.

Stepping away from her, I put my hands behind my back, afraid she might hurt me. How did I not recognize her before? Even with the red hair, her face looked the same as the picture. And her eyes—pure green—the mark of a Pure.

"She repelled Tavion with her blood," Farrell explained.

I couldn't make eye contact with Ms. Ryken or Farrell. If I did, they'd see the hurt, and I wanted to keep that to myself. "You don't know me," I said. "Neither of you do. Now please, leave me alone."

I dragged my tired and beaten body upstairs. My neck throbbed, my hands ached, and I needed a shower. When I stepped into the hot water, I winced. The stream hurt every inch of me. When

I put the soap in my hands, I almost yelled. But my hurt was nothing compared to what had happened to Trent and Veronica.

She died because of me.

My battered body sank to the bottom of the tub. That's when I lost it. Every emotion spilled out of me. I didn't fight the tears. I didn't try to be strong. I let myself cry until each tear in my body released.

After a while, the hot water turned cold. When I got out of the shower, I dried off, wrapped my hands as best as I could, and sat on my bed in the dark. I texted my parents and even left them messages, but got no response. Were they okay? And then I thought of the feather Ms. Ryken, or Colleen, or whoever she was, had given me. I tore open my bag, flung everything out, and grabbed the book where I had put the feather. I held it tight. *Please, be in there.* I flipped through the pages, slowly at first and then with quick desperation. It was gone! Lost! I chucked the book at the wall, when the doorbell rang. My body tensed.

"Dominique," Farrell called out. "It's Infiniti."

I knew, without a doubt, that she had come over because of Veronica. When I got to the door, I found her face red and covered in tears. "She's… she's… dead. Veronica is… dead."

I held Infiniti while she cried in my arms.

CHAPTER *Sixteen*

WITH CHRISTMAS GETTING CLOSER, AND my birthday, or death day, on the horizon, a permanent sense of dread had settled deep inside me. Mom and Dad had called to check on me and said they'd be back by Christmas day. They also told me that Ms. Ryken, or Colleen, was a Pure like them and had reinforced my shield. Even though they thought Tavion had been wounded enough to give us a reprieve, they ordered me not to leave the house. But when I told them about Veronica and a candlelight vigil Infiniti had prepared for her, they said I could go because they knew I would anyway.

Infiniti had planned the memorial at our neighborhood lake. Even though Veronica wasn't my favorite person, she didn't deserve to die because of me. Nobody deserved to have their life cut short like that. I went to Infiniti's to help her get ready.

"I should've been there for her," Infiniti said. Her face was pale, her hair a thick tangled mess.

Dark, puffy circles hung from her eyes. She smelled like she had spent most of the day smoking.

I took a brush from her dresser and started working on her locks. "You were there for her, Infiniti. You were a good friend to her, and wherever she is, she knows it."

She dotted concealer under her eyes and began rubbing it in. "You think so?"

"Yes, I do." Of course, I wasn't exactly sure if I was right or not, but I had to believe that I was. Veronica was an innocent victim of Tavion. Wherever she was, she had to be at peace. Infiniti sat silently while I tried to make sense of her knotted hair.

"How about we put your hair up? That might be easier."

She handed me a rubber band. "I hate my hair," she said sullenly.

When I pulled it up, it actually looked pretty good. "Are you crazy? Your hair is gorgeous and you're beautiful. Women pay hundreds of dollars to have hair half as amazing as yours."

She looked at me through the mirror with puppy dog brown eyes. "Thanks, Dominique. I don't know what I'd do without you."

I avoided her glance. If Tavion had his way, I'd be dead soon, and then she'd have to live through the death of another friend. It wasn't fair—none of it was. I glanced at her desk clock.

"It's almost six. Ready to go?"

With a nod she got up, put on her black coat, grabbed a box of candles, and together we headed to the lake. Halfway down the street, Billy

153

showed up. He parked and came over to us. His normally bright and freckled face had lost all its color. He hugged Infiniti and cried on her shoulder. Then the three of us linked arms and continued on to the lake.

Infiniti had texted as many people as she could about Veronica's lakeside gathering. When we got to the lake, we found a huge crowd of people. Infiniti and Billy made their way through the throng, hugging and crying with their friends. And then I saw Trent. He looked… normal. Like nothing had happened to him. I had no idea how much of his memory Farrell had erased, but apparently he didn't remember that I was supposedly dating Farrell, that we had kissed at Infiniti's, or that we had been attacked at a red desert because he came up to me and gave me a hug.

"Man, I can't believe what happened to Veronica," he said. "How's Infiniti taking it?"

I shivered from the cool December air that intensified with the setting sun. "She's holding up okay. You know — as well as can be expected."

Infiniti handed out candles to those who hadn't brought any. The glowing sea of lights lit up the entire area. She stood on top of the bench and started talking about her friendship with Veronica. While highlighting all the fun times they had, guilt settled in me. Did their friendship suffer because of me? I hoped not. And then I thought of Tavion. Her death was his fault. Not mine. He had killed her. At least, that's what I told myself.

When Infiniti finished, Billy took the bench, followed by others who shared their Veronica memories. Lost in their tales, a newfound admiration for Veronica grew inside me, when a figure on the other side of the lake caught my eye. It was getting dark, but the setting sun cast out streaks of light that revealed a tall woman with a long skirt and shoulder-length blond hair—it had to be Jan. I slipped through the crowd and hurried in her direction.

Please, Jan, let that be you. As soon as the path curved to the right, I saw a white feather on the ground. Standing right by it was Jan. I exhaled, relieved to find her okay and alive.

"Jan, it's so good to see you. I thought you were..." I didn't want to say that I thought she was dead. "Never mind, I'm really glad to see you."

"My dear, I told you I would come back," she said in her vibrating voice. "Come, let's walk."

Before I took a step, I noticed the white feather had vanished. Or maybe it really wasn't there? I wasn't sure, but I was glad to have Jan back. We walked in silence for a while along the narrow jogging path. A gust of wind swept through the tall pines and flowed right past us. When it did, vanilla filled the air.

"How was your trip?" I asked.

Our shoes crunched on the gravel. Her eyes drifted up to the near-dark sky. "It was fine."

Her answer didn't sound very reassuring. "That's good. Did you find out anything about my mark? About what's happening to me?"

She stopped in her tracks. The cool wind that whipped around us faded. "No. I'm sorry, dear. But I can tell you this," she added. "You must go to midnight mass with Trent."

My skin crawled with shivers. Had I told her about his invitation? I couldn't remember. I was about to ask when Trent called out for me in the distance.

"Sounds like someone's looking for you," she said.

My eyes stayed on Jan's. "But Jan," I pleaded. "I need your help."

"I know, my dear, and I'm truly sorry. I wish I could offer you more assistance, but I can't right now. Perhaps later."

Later? Later I could be dead. Didn't she care? My stomach tightened and I forced the lump in my throat to stay down. I couldn't speak, so I settled on a nod.

She reached out to touch me, but stopped short. "I must go now, but I *will* see you again." Her emphasis on the word will puzzled me, but then again, much about her confused me. "I wish you well, Dominique."

"Thank you, Jan."

She walked away, leaving me in a daze. I started back toward the crowd when I thought of the book Abigail had given me, the journal of Julian Huxley. I wondered if Jan knew something about it. I spun around to ask, but she was gone. She should have still been on the path, but wasn't. Goose bumps ran up and down my spine.

"Dominique!" Trent called out again.

I wrapped myself in my jacket and made my way back to the vigil. The ceremony had ended, but several people had stayed around. I didn't see Farrell, but knew he had to be close.

"Hey," Trent said. "Where'd you go?"

"Down the path, chatting with one of my neighbors."

He sat on a bench, the same bench where he found me the night my parents had told me they were Transhumans and my life was in danger. It wasn't long ago, but it felt like forever. Exhausted, I sat beside him.

He put his arm around me and noticed my bandaged hands. "What happened?"

Scenes from the confrontation in the red desert flashed through my mind. "Nothing. Cut myself cooking."

"Seriously?" he asked, half smiling at me. "Cooking?"

"Yep, cooking," I answered with a small laugh because it was such a lame excuse. "I'm not much of a cook."

"Well, I'm a great one," he said, hugging me. "So if you ever need to make something, don't. Call me instead and I'll come over."

Everything about Trent made me comfortable. Being near him made me think I could be normal, even though I knew I couldn't.

"You can still come with me and my grandmother to Christmas Eve midnight mass, right?'

I thought of Jan's advice for me to go with Trent to mass, and how his grandmother had said that mass was where they Pures go. Jan's directive and *Abuela's* words couldn't have been a coincidence. I hoped my parents would let me go.

"I'm pretty sure I can go. If you still want me to that is."

"Of course I want you to come." He gave me a squeeze. The fresh scent of soap filled the air and relaxed me. "I gotta go to work. How about I pick you up at eight?"

"Sure, see you then."

When he left, Infiniti joined me on the bench. She leaned her head on my shoulder, and we sat in the cold, staring out at the lake. It was completely dark, save for the glow from the half-moon that hung overhead and the light from the fountain in the middle of the lake. It lit up with different colors: green, purple, and then red. The water cascaded out and splashed into the rippling lake. The sounds made me think of the beach back home and the place I had been transported to when I had touched the feather, and then again when Tavion had almost killed me — the place with Farrell.

I looked around for him, but didn't see him. Everyone had left except for Infiniti and me. I was about to suggest we go in when her phone beeped. She sat up and read the text. She dropped her phone. Her body froze. She stared straight ahead and didn't say a word.

"Infiniti, what is it?"

"Jan. Is. Dead."

CHAPTER *Seventeen*

THEY SAY DEATH COMES IN threes. The first death? Veronica, an innocent bystander killed at the hand of Tavion. A death explained as a car crash. The second? Jan, reported as killed when her plane crashed during her flight from Oracle to Houston. But I knew Tavion had killed her, too. The third? That was going to be me.

Even though Farrell had said the end was not yet written, I didn't think I had a chance. Somehow I needed to change that, but how? It was one day before Christmas Eve. Mom and Dad had said they'd be home, but weren't yet. When I pressed Farrell for their whereabouts, he said they'd tell me when they got home. The secrecy killed me, but he insisted it was necessary for my safety. How could I argue with that?

Hardly sleeping and barely eating, I decided enough was enough. When I burst into Farrell's room to tell him we needed to formulate a plan, he tried to convince me to wait for my parents, but I wouldn't let him. After a heated argument, he reluctantly came around to my way of thinking.

A few key things were working in our favor: my blood somehow harmed Tavion, Abigail was an ally, and the journal of Julian Huxley contained answers. Mom and Dad had the book, but the rest of his writings were at the Rice library.

"I'm sick of waiting around," I said. "I know you are too, Farrell. I can tell. I say we go back to the school. We need to read as much as we can on Julian Huxley."

Farrell paced the room for a minute before he answered. "Fine."

We got to the college before ten and found the campus quiet and empty. All the students were home, getting ready for Christmas—a time for family, food, and presents. I envied them because for me Christmas was now a time of death, despair, and fear.

Farrell and I walked through the tall, sand-colored stone archway that took us from the front of the school to the quad. As we walked, Farrell's hand brushed against mine. I thought of all the times Farrell had filled my mind. I knew there had to have been something between us in our past lives.

"You really don't remember any of our past lives?" I asked, hoping that maybe he did.

He slowed his pace. "No, none of us do."

"Are you sure?" I asked, stopping and getting in front of him. Every mark from his confrontation with Tavion had disappeared. He had explained it as a power to heal. My wounds remained, and my hands were still stiff and achy.

"Yes," he said. "I'm sure. Now, come on. Let's get what we need and get out of here."

He was right; we needed to hurry. We started for the library when a crackle of lightning filled the air in front of us. I shielded my eyes. When I lowered them, I saw the same Tracker as before— tall, lean, and dressed in black. The one who had found Farrell and me the first time we were here.

Farrell gathered his white and yellow-hued aura in his hands, ready to strike the Tracker.

The Tracker quickly raised his arms. "I have a message for the Marked One."

My stomach tightened, my heart raced. Farrell backed down. The energy in his hands faded.

"Speak," Farrell said.

The Tracker relaxed his stance and stepped closer. He stood eye to eye with Farrell. They had almost the exact same build and features. The main difference was their hair color. While Farrell's was blond, the Tracker's was black.

"Tavion sends word." The Tracker raised his hand. His gray mist trickled out until it formed a thin oval-shaped mass in front of us. It was almost like a gray window, but instead of reflecting us, it showed an image. It was fuzzy at first, and then I made out my mom and dad. Mom lay on the ground, her eyes closed. Dad paced back and forth, his clothes tattered and burned, his face cut and bleeding. My stomach lurched. I grabbed Farrell's arm.

The Tracker's eyes fixed on Farrell. "Tavion will release Caris and Stone upon surrender of the Marked One. Said surrender and exchange to occur in three days."

For a minute there, I didn't know who the Tracker was referring to since I wasn't used to hearing my parents called by their first names.

The Tracker's glare landed on me. "If the Marked One refuses, Caris and Stone will be extinguished and the Marked One hunted and killed. You have thirty seconds to decide."

Terror soared through my veins. My heart exploded with fear. I couldn't let anything happen to my mom and dad—I just couldn't. Farrell turned his back on the Tracker and brought his face close to mine. "Dominique, I am charged with your safety. Your parents know this. They would not want you to sacrifice yourself for them. Not ever. The balance of good and evil, the future of this world, depends on your survival."

My attention stayed on my parents. Farrell placed his hands my shoulders. "Do you hear me? You must refuse. You must not surrender."

Yes, I heard him, but I couldn't accept what he had to say. There was no way I could give up my parents like that. Especially since all their lives, for nine lifetimes now, they had protected me. Besides, if I surrendered, I would have three days to come up with something. There had to be another way.

My pulse quickened. I didn't even know I was biting the inside of my mouth until I tasted blood. "I surrender!"

Farrell's green eyes widened with disbelief, his hands still locked on my shoulders. "What have you done?" he whispered. He released me and stared down at the ground. Shock covered his face. Before turning to face the Tracker, he erased the disappointment and stood tall. "Tell Tavion we'll be ready for surrender in three days at the place of our choosing when the moon is at its peak." He lifted his hand. His aura trickled out of his fingers. "And no harm shall befall Caris or Stone. If it does, I will find you and kill you."

The Tracker narrowed his eyes at Farrell. Then he looked at me. "The Marked One has spoken. In three days the Marked One will exchange her life for her parents." The misty image of my parents disappeared, and so did the Tracker.

An uncomfortable and thick silence engulfed Farrell and me. I knew he was pissed, but he didn't say anything. Instead, he continued on to the library.

"Hey," I said. "Don't you want to talk about my surrender? Come up with a way to get out of it? I mean, you're my protector and all, right?"

He kept a fast pace. "There's no getting out of a surrender."

I gulped. "Well, what then? There must be something we can do. We have three days." Instead of answering me, he continued walking. I ran past him and stopped in his path. "Farrell! Stop! I'm trying to talk to you!"

He rubbed his face and sat on a nearby cement bench. "You are very hard to protect, Dominique, did you know that?"

This whole time I hadn't thought about Farrell and what it must be like to protect me. I had touched those cards that first exposed my energy to the Tainted. I played the Ouija board and had almost gotten myself and Infiniti killed. Then, as if one near-death experience weren't enough, I went back for the board that Veronica ended up having and used in my house, which later led to her death and almost mine and Trent's. Now I had surrendered to the enemy. He probably thought I had a death wish.

"I'm sorry, Farrell. I'm not trying to be difficult."

He ran his fingers through his hair. "I know. But here we are with your parents captured, three days before your surrender, and we have no idea how to defeat Tavion."

So I wouldn't make it to my eighteenth birthday after all. Not even New Year's Eve. "Listen, Farrell, there are benefits to knowing when I'm supposed to die. I mean, now there's no more waiting on edge, worrying all day, sleepless nights. When you think of it, for once we have the advantage. We know when Tavion will strike. We can even pick the place. That's gotta count for something, right?"

"We shall see."

Farrell and I slipped into the library the same way as before, by using his energy to dissolve the glass wall. Once inside, we scanned the area to make sure we were alone. The air smelled like new carpet. It was overpowering at first, but gradually, I got used to it. The white walls were plain, save for a few books that were opened and hung like pieces of art, books I hadn't noticed before. There was even a stack of books up against two walls made to look like trees.

"Back here," Farrell said.

We zigzagged our way through the long, white cubicle style desks. As we did, I noticed the books on the walls had shadowy figures on them — birds. The artwork on each book had birds, and a few of the books were made to look like they were flying from one tree to the other. I swallowed, searching the floor, thinking I might see a white feather, but didn't.

When we got to a back room, we found it empty. I grabbed my hair and began twisting, panic taking me over again. "This is where they were, right?"

Farrell brought my hand down. "Let's check the library computer. Maybe the school moved the documents."

Two clear signs hung above a long, white desk with two computers: REFERENCE. Farrell turned the computer on with a wave of his hand. I thought for sure there'd be a password or something on there, but Farrell managed to go directly to his search, his abilities by passing any online security. He typed "Julian Huxley Documents." Pages and pages of documents filled the screen. The status of each? Checked out.

"Oh, hell," I said, tingling shivers erupting inside me. "Somebody knew we were coming."

"Maybe," he said. He typed "Julian Huxley Transhumanism." Up popped the paper Julian Huxley wrote in 1956. I was surprised to see that it wasn't that long. Farrell printed it. Then, I leaned over Farrell and typed "Julian Huxley Biography."

A history of the public figure filled the screen. I read out loud. "Julian Huxley was born in England in 1887. A brilliant scientist with a keen mind for discovery, he often had serious and debilitating attacks of depression. He taught at Oxford but left in 1913 to teach biology at the new Rice Institute in Houston, Texas. He stayed at Rice from 1913 until 1916. He left and returned to Europe to take part in WWI."

Huxley's bio went on and on with his teachings, his writings, and his associations, when something caught my interest. "Check this out." I pointed at the screen. "In 1929, he left his wife and returned to the United States. He left no account of his life at that time, but eventually returned to England in 1931. Farrell, that's two years of silence."

Farrell pushed his chair back. "That's during the time of his journal, right?"

"Yes," I said. "The journal was dated 1930."

Farrell muttered. "One year before he returned to England." He went to the printer and retrieved the paper on Transhumanism. "This paper is dated 1957. So whatever happened here in the States could have, and probably did, directly influence the writing of this paper."

"Abigail," I said. "He found her here and studied her. She's the key." The quiet library echoed the stillness. "We either need that journal, or we need to somehow communicate with her," I said. "If we don't, we lose."

Jan had seen Abigail in a school back in Arizona. I had seen her in my house, in my parents' study. She was a Transhuman, an ancient energy being like Farrell and my parents, and somehow Huxley had found her in the United States.

"Farrell, when Abigail brought me Huxley's journal, you said that when Huxley wrote about

Transhumanism, he was actually writing about you guys, right?"

"Yes, that's right."

"And he knew about Transhumans because he found Abigail and he studied her, right?"

"Yes."

"But you also said that somehow she had died. Well, how exactly does someone like Abigail, a Transhuman, die?"

"Energy, once created, can never be destroyed. It can only be relocated or transformed."

"What?" I asked. "Relocated? Transformed? So she's not dead?"

He crumpled up a piece of paper. "Think of it this way. This is a regular sheet of paper that people use every day." He closed his hand tight around the ball. A glow came from inside his hand. The smell of burning paper filled the air. Black smoke trickled through his fingers. When he opened his hand, the paper had turned to black clumps. "See, it's still the same paper, but it's been transformed to ash."

"So she's ash?" I thought of people who get cremated when they die, and I shivered.

"Not exactly. In her case, as with all Transhumans, the only way we die is to get relocated, or absorbed by another energy source."

"Hold on," I said. "Absorbed?" Even though I asked, I knew exactly what he meant. Tavion's hand had dissolved into my chest when he had me trapped in that vapor bubble in the red desert. He called it taking my energy source.

"Yes—absorbed, taken, one energy source taking another," Farrell explained. "That's what

Tavion was doing to you in that red desert. He was draining your energy. And that's what he'll do to you when you turn yourself over in three days." Farrell paused for a minute. He leaned forward in his chair. "Dominique, I don't think you get it. When he absorbs your energy source, you die. Tavion and the Tainted win. Game over for mankind."

Farrell and my parents had told me that my death would bring about some sort of destruction, but I didn't realize exactly what kind until now. Tavion's hollow, pale, and creepy face flashed before my eyes.

My death would turn the world into hell.

CHAPTER
Eighteen

I WAS BEGINNING TO THINK dying was better than living. At least, my kind of living—always on edge, afraid of shadows in the night, guilt-ridden over the deaths of two people, responsible for the capture of my parents. My surrender couldn't come fast enough.

Farrell and I had stayed at the library until morning, but didn't find anything to help us. We figured the answers were in Julian Huxley's journal, but my parents had it and Tavion had them. Even though Farrell remained optimistic, I couldn't. I couldn't even fake it. And when Christmas Eve arrived, my despair only multiplied. Christmas Eve was a time for celebration—a religious holiday of birth. For me it was just one step closer to death. And even though I should've been excited about seeing Trent later, I could barely even think about him and our date.

Farrell stayed in his room most of the day while I stayed in mine, scribbling notes of everything that had happened to me since moving here. So many things crammed my mind, but three stood out more than the rest—the image of my captive parents, the sight of Abigail holding Julian Huxley's journal, and Farrell's words at the library.

The only way we die is to get relocated, or absorbed by another energy source.

Those words echoed in my head until I thought I might go crazy. And then, I got it! Tavion wanted to absorb my energy, but what if we absorbed his first? I flung off my blanket, raced down the hall, and burst into Farrell's room. He was kneeling on the floor by his bed, head down. His hands covered his heart while his body radiated a yellow glow that filled the room like a soft sun. As if sensing my interruption, the glow expanded, blasting like a thousand sun rays. I shielded my eyes. When the light faded, I brought my hands down, but couldn't see anything. Everything had gone black. Farrell's warm and tingly hands cupped my face. "Dominique, I'm so sorry. I didn't hear you coming in. Are you okay?"

A vibration spread through my cheeks and filtered throughout my body. Warmth filled me, and a longing for him. My sight littered with splotches of darkness that eventually started to fade. He ushered me to his bed. I didn't want to sit down, but he forced me.

"Farrell, I'm all right, really." My sight started to normalize. "What were you doing?"

"In two days you're supposed to surrender to Tavion," he said. "But I'm not going to let him have you, Dominique. I'll die before that happens."

My stomach tightened. "Farrell, that's what happened in each lifetime before, isn't it? You died trying to protect me."

He studied my eyes. "Yes," he said. "We all died."

Dizziness overcame me and I forced myself to breathe deep. I needed to focus on solutions. "Farrell, you said that Tavion was going to absorb my energy, right? Well, I had a thought. What if we absorb his first?"

He tilted his head to the side and considered my words. "That's not possible for you. You don't have the right energy source."

My hopes sank. Maybe there was no way out of my death. Maybe it was inevitable.

"But I have the right energy," he added.

I swallowed hard. "If you absorb Tavion's energy, what will happen? Will you be okay?"

He rubbed his hands on his jeans. "I don't know. A Pure has never absorbed the energy of a Tainted. It's one thing that separates us from them."

Before I could say anything else, he walked to the door. "It's almost seven. You better get ready."

Farrell and I had argued about me going with Trent and his grandmother to midnight mass. He didn't want me to go because my parents had ordered me to stay with him. But because Jan had said I should go, he reluctantly agreed. We couldn't pass up an opportunity for clues.

I had never been to church before, and I had no idea what to wear. I scanned the dresses in my closet—settling on two that might work. One was a tight-fitting black sleeveless dress that hung right above my knees. The other was dark purple with thick straps and a low neckline. It too was short, but not as short as the black dress. I laid both out on my bed, slipped on my black heels, and held each in front of the mirror.

The black one looked too sexy, the purple one was more conservative, more churchy. And so I picked the purple. Dressed and finished with my hair and makeup, I stepped back and studied myself. Not bad for someone who hadn't slept well in weeks. I hoped it wasn't too much, yet at the same time I hoped it was enough to make an impression. For all I knew, this could be my last night out ever and I wanted to look my best.

I draped my black wrap around my shoulders, when the doorbell rang. I forced myself to take a few deep breaths before I grabbed my purse and the small gift I had for Trent.

When I got downstairs, I found Trent and Farrell by the door—silent. Farrell had shoved his hands in his jean pockets, his face serious. Trent had polished away his messy exterior. He wore a black suit with a white shirt and a slender red tie. The only trace of messiness was his hair.

"Wow," he said. "Dominique, you look amazing."

Heat filtered through my cheeks. "Thanks. You too," I said, avoiding Farrell's gaze, which I could tell, had glued on me since coming downstairs.

Trent took my hand. "You ready?'

"Yes," I said.

"What time will you be home?" Farrell asked.

I let Trent answer since I had no idea how

long midnight mass would take. "I'll have her home around two." Then Trent looked at me. "So, is he in charge or something?"

Farrell crossed his arms. Before he could say anything to Trent, I offered a quick explanation. "No, it's not like that. But my parents are out of town on business, and he doesn't want to worry." I fidgeted. "Right, Farrell?"

Farrell clenched his jaw before answering. "Right."

Trent wrapped his arm around my waist. "Don't worry. I'll take good care of her."

It was the worst thing he could've said to Farrell, and it made me feel horrible. Farrell didn't deserve a jab like that.

The ride to Trent's was short and quiet. My stomach twisted tight. My mind kept replaying my conversation with Jan, or at least, the ghost of Jan back at the trail on the lake. She had said I needed to go to midnight mass with Trent, but why?

My deep thoughts were interrupted by Trent's decked out house. The quaint cottage sparkled with hundreds of white Christmas lights. They reminded me of hope, of life. Unlike mine, which had no light. No hope.

Trent parked the car in the driveway and waited a moment. "You okay, Dominique? You seem a little off."

Off? If only he knew. "I'm fine. Just a little nervous, I guess. I'm not really a church person."

He touched my shoulder. "Don't worry. I'll be right beside you the whole time."

"I know you will. Thanks, Trent." I put on a

reassuring smile. "Come on. Let's not keep your grandmother waiting."

When we walked into the house, the festive scene immediately calmed my nerves. The Christmas tree twinkled with tiny white lights. Spanish holiday music played softly in the background. The aroma of something savory and delicious wafted my way. My mouth watered.

"Mmmm, what's on the menu?" I asked.

"My grandmother's chili and tamales. It's our traditional Christmas Eve dinner."

We walked into the kitchen and found his grandmother cleaning up. She wore a blue dress with a pink flower pinned to her lapel. Her hair twisted up in a tight little bun, and she wore the same silver rosary I had seen before.

"*Abuela*, Dominique is here."

She smiled. "Hello, *Mija*. Thank you for coming. Please, sit."

I sat at the small, wooden table while Trent's grandmother worked her way around the kitchen with ease. She served us each a bowl of chili and a plate of tamales. Trent gathered the silverware, napkins, and drinks.

"This looks wonderful," I said as they sat down.

"Thank you, *Mija*. Now let's bless our food."

She and Trent held out their hands. Nervous to take theirs because of my bandaged wounds and because I had never prayed before, I hesitated. Trent opened one eye, took my hand, and nodded for me to take his grandmother's.

"It's okay," he mouthed.

I slowly reached out for her. When our hands

touched, his grandmother shuddered, squeezed tight, and started praying fast, as if her life depended on it.

"Dear Lord, please bless us on this the eve of the birth of your son. Bless your daughter, Dominique, and be with her as she walks into a dark place, a place that, dear Lord, only you can help her get through. Let her be brave and strong. In the name of your son, Jesus Christ. Amen."

She drew her hand away and stared straight ahead at nothing. Completely freaked out, I wanted to get up and leave. Trent placed his hand over mine reassuringly, yet he wore a somewhat confused look on his face.

His grandmother interrupted our exchange. "Let us enjoy this time." She picked up her spoon, and started eating. "Come," she urged. "I didn't cook all day for nothing!"

Her humor relaxed me a little, so I picked up my spoon, too, as did Trent. When the chili hit my mouth, an explosion of flavors filled my taste buds. The broth had chunks of meat and tomatoes with little bits of onion and celery. It was spicy, but not too spicy.

Trent scooped up a spoonful of chili and poured it over his tamales. "Try it like this."

I did the same and took a bite. The tamales were amazing, and I ate every last bite. I even thought of asking for seconds when it dawned on me that I hadn't eaten that much in a long time.

After we finished our meal, Trent's grandmother excused herself. "Save room for my *tres leches*, both of you," she said with a smile. "I'll be right back."

"There's always room for *tres leches*," Trent said to me playfully, scooting his chair closer to mine, our knees touching.

"I guess, if I knew what is was," I said with a smile.

"What?" he asked, flabbergasted. "There's no *tres leches* up north?"

"Not that I'm aware of."

He played with my fingers while we talked. "It's a Mexican cake made with three different types of milk. *Tres* means three, *leches* means milk. You'll love it!"

I found myself playing with his fingers, too. "If your grandmother made it, then I'm sure I will."

His blue eyes studied mine for a while. He leaned close. For a second there I thought he might kiss me, but he didn't.

"I want to show you something," he said.

We got up and he led me to the Christmas tree. He knelt down to retrieve a medium-sized box wrapped in silver paper with a large red ribbon. He handed it to me. "For you."

I unwrapped the gift to find a snow globe. Inside was a tiny village. I shook the globe gently. Tiny snowflakes fell on the town. It was beautiful — and I was speechless.

"I've never been to Elk Rapids," he said. "But this globe reminded me of it."

He was right. It was exactly like Elk Rapids — small, peaceful, serene. How I missed it there. My eyes started to water as I gazed at the village. It reminded me of everything I was about to lose.

"I'm sorry." He wrapped his arms around me.

"I didn't mean to upset you."

I shook my head. "Don't be sorry, Trent. I love it. It's perfect. Thank you so much."

He pulled me close for a tender embrace. I held him tight, almost afraid to let go. He whispered in my ear. "You sure you're okay?"

I held him to me before I answered. "I'm fine."

After a moment, I let go and regained my composure. "Now it's your turn." I took my purse from the couch, reached in, and pulled out a small box I had wrapped in brown paper.

Trent opened it and pulled out a Petoskey Stone I had found and polished when I was little. He eyed it admiringly.

"Dominique, this is amazing. What kind of stone is it?"

My mind took me back to all the afternoons I had spent with my dad at Deep Water Point. We would comb the shallow part of the bay for hours looking for Petoskey Stones. We used to come home with handfuls of treasures. For months, we polished the stones until they transformed from ordinary rocks to shiny treasures.

"It's a Petoskey Stone, the state stone of Michigan. The stones were once living coral that existed millions of years ago. Over time, the coral fossilized and glaciers scattered the stones along Lake Michigan. When found, they're gray and rough, but when polished, like this one, the coral pattern emerges."

Trent ran his fingers over the stone, admiring its shape and the imprints on the surface. I knew he would like it. It was so him, somewhat rugged at first glance, yet so amazing when its true qualities were exposed.

"I'll think of you every time I look at it." He pulled me closer and was about to kiss me when we heard his grandmother's shuffling footsteps coming down the hallway. We separated slowly.

"Are you two ready for dessert?" she asked.

"We're ready if you are," he said, still holding my fingers.

"Good, we don't want to be late for mass," she said. "But first, I have something for you, Dominique."

My eyes went wide. "Me?"

"Yes, *Mija*," she said, handing me a small white jewelry box. "This has been in my family for generations, and I want you to have it."

I looked at Trent, wondering if he knew about the gift. He raised his shoulders and shook his head, as surprised as me.

"*Abuela*, you shouldn't have," I said.

When I opened it, I found a silver necklace with a cross shaped stone that also resembled a sword. A familiar vibration filled my fingertips when I touched it. I brought it closer. It was black with red and green flecks—a bloodstone. The stone that called to me at Jan's; a stone that soldiers took to battle. Is this why Jan had wanted me to go to mass with Trent and his grandmother? So Trent's grandmother could give me this necklace?

"It's beautiful," I said. "Thank you so much."

"The cross will remind you to have faith. The sword shape will remind you to be strong," she explained.

I took the cross out of the box and handed it to Trent so he could put it on me. The silver chain felt cool on my skin, while the stone felt warm.

"It looks great on you," Trent said.

"Good, I knew it would," his grandmother said. "Now let's have dessert, and then we'll go."

The white *tres leches* cake was scrumptious—spongy but not soggy, with a light fluffy frosting. But my stomach had twisted tight again, and I could only have a few bites. Trent's grandmother's gift meant something, but what? That I needed faith and strength? That I would win? And did Jan know that Trent's grandmother would give it to me?

There were too many unknowns in my life, and thinking about them made me crazy. But this was my path; this was where I needed to be. Maybe I would find a clue at church. After all, that's where people pray for answers.

CHAPTER
Nineteen

Trent had explained that we were going to St. Joseph's Catholic Church in a historical district nestled near downtown Houston. Butterflies filled my stomach during the twenty-minute drive from our neighborhood on the northwest side to the heart of Houston that littered with skyscrapers. When we approached, I was surprised to find a small, red brick church, not grand like the churches you read about in history class. But at the same time, it looked old, as if it had been there for a long while.

"The church was built in 1880. My parents got married here, and so did my grandparents," Trent said as we walked to the entrance.

When we entered the church, its understated yet grand beauty struck me. Magnificent columns lined both sides of the interior walls. They were a crisp white, adorned with leaves and scrolls at the top. The walls were a slightly darker ivory, allowing the architectural detail of the columns to stand out.

Trent's grandmother placed a black, lace scarf over her head and then kneeled. After she rose, she placed her fingers in a bowl of water in the center of the foyer. She made the sign of the cross up and down her chest. Trent kneeled and did the same with the water.

As we walked down the aisle to the front of the church, I noticed a series of art pieces lining the walls. "What are those?" I whispered to Trent.

"The Stations of the Cross. The pictures tell the story of the crucifixion of Jesus. Let's get our seats, and then I'll show you."

After putting our things down on a pew at the front, Trent whispered to his grandmother that he was going to show me around. She nodded, and knelt down in prayer. It was interesting to see her completely shrouded in tradition. When I looked around, I saw other Hispanic ladies with their heads covered with the same type of lacey scarves. Some were black, others were white.

"Those are mantillas," Trent whispered, catching on to my curiosity right away. "Married women and widows wear the black, unmarried women wear the white. It's a tradition, and a symbol of respect for the church."

He took my hand and led me to the back of the church to the artwork I had asked about. He called each piece a station and explained them to me in detail one by one. When we got to the seventh station, I was surprised to see it damaged and burnt.

"What happened to that one?"

"The Church caught on fire in 1995. They restored each station except this one, which serves as a reminder of how delicate life is." Trent eyed the piece. "This is the seventh station where Jesus fell for the second time when carrying the cross to Calvary, the place of his crucifixion."

How delicate life is. I thought of my life and the uncertainty that plagued me. I had fallen too, but eight times. Would this time be any different? I would know in two days. I thought of the pain when Tavion had plunged his hand into me and said he was taking my energy source. My hand lighted on my chest. I didn't know if I could take that pain again.

Trent waited patiently, allowing me to explore my thoughts. "Will you let me in there one of these days?"

"Into my thoughts?"

"Your thoughts, your heart, everything."

Heat crept up my cheeks. Every inch of me told me that Farrell had meant something to me in our past lives, though neither one of us remembered it. But was I destined to be with Farrell? Or Trent? And for that matter, could I ever be normal again?

"Maybe," I said.

Trent leaned in. "I'll take maybe. For now."

He took my hand and led me back up the aisle to our seats. His confident and warm grip eased me. Nothing would happen to me here, I thought. When we sat, a deep silence engulfed the church. After a while, an organ started playing and a beautiful choir filled the air. The voices were perfectly tuned, harmoniously intertwined, and rich with depth.

My eyes scanned the church, searching for

the source. Trent pointed behind us and up. The balcony was filled with people in white robes standing before a massive organ. The church had packed with people, too. The music stopped. In its place, loud and triumphant church bells chimed. When the bells finished, choir music filled the air again. Everyone stood while five priests in magnificent white robes with gold trim and tall ornate hats walked down the center aisle. Trent had been thoughtful enough to let me sit by the aisle so I could see everything.

One of the priests swung a large gold incense holder by a chain. It reminded me of the smell of Infiniti's room, earthy and magical. With each stride, he swung it back and forth. The powerful scent made my eyes water and my throat itch. My head started to spin. I clutched my hands together, afraid I might faint.

Please, don't faint here. I closed my eyes in an attempt to steady my head. When I opened them, the aisle had almost cleared, with only one final person left in the procession. It was a young girl. When she came to our row, she stopped. I sucked in my breath, my heart beating wildly. I recognized her white dress, long white hair, and big green eyes.

"Abigail," I whispered.

"Yes," she answered with a steady and clear voice. Her face glowed with a radiant, soft pink light.

I glanced around and realized that no one else saw her or heard her but me. I wondered if I was hallucinating, but when I blinked, she was still there, her eyes focused on me alone.

"Dominique, my message is true. You must find the journal hidden by your parents in the ocean by the tree. And you must stay with Farrell. He will protect you from what is coming. You must have faith. You must be strong. And you must know that Julian Huxley did not nothing wrong."

Huxley did nothing wrong? My parents had hidden the journal? All along, Farrell and I thought they had taken it with them, believing that Tavion now had it. But Abigail was telling me something else.

Have faith and be strong… I knew those words. Trent's grandmother had used them when she gave me the necklace.

Abigail reached out. I flinched as she placed her tiny fingertips on my cross. She closed her eyes. The soft glow around her face intensified until a tingly feeling flooded my body and left me lightheaded.

She opened her eyes. "Do not be afraid." She tilted her head to the side and stared at Trent. She smiled. "I knew you'd find my friend."

My head continued spinning out of control. I knew I was about to faint, but I didn't want to. How could she and Trent possibly be friends? My vision dimmed, my body swayed, and before I could ask her, darkness surrounded me.

WHEN I OPENED MY EYES, I found myself on a couch. A wet and cool cloth draped over my forehead. I blinked, adjusting my eyes to the artificial lighting overhead.

"Hey, there." It was Trent. He had taken off his jacket and tie and studied me with a worry-filled look.

"Where am I? What happened?"

"We're in a church office. You fainted right after the procession, and we carried you here."

I sat up, and immediately my head started spinning again. Trent held me to him. "Whoa, slow down."

"I'm so sorry, Trent. I didn't mean to ruin your night. I know how much this mass means to you and your grandmother." I searched the room for her.

"She's in the church," he said. "And you didn't ruin anything. I secretly wanted you all to myself anyway."

I rested my head on his shoulder and held him tight. He smelled clean and fresh, and being so close to him sent a warm feeling throughout me.

"Really?" I whispered.

He cradled the back of my head with a strong and steady hand. "Yes, really."

After a moment, he pulled away and studied my face intently. "Are you sure you're okay?"

I thought of Abigail, her words and her touch. I brought my hand to my cross. Energy still pulsated from it. What did it mean? I could never ask Trent; he'd think me crazy. Then my mind filled with Farrell. I almost thought of calling out to him, but stopped myself.

"I guess all the incense got to me."

He smiled. "I should've warned you. Catholics love their incense, especially at midnight mass." Then, becoming serious, he added, "We don't have to go back in. We can wait here until the mass is over."

"No, I'm okay. I want to go back." I didn't want to ruin the evening for him anymore than I already had. Plus, I wanted to see if I might catch another glimpse of Abigail.

"Okay, we'll go back. But I am not letting go of your hand, and if you feel lightheaded, give a squeeze and we'll leave. Okay?"

"Okay."

He took my hand and led me back to our seats. While we walked, I searched for Abigail, but she was gone. Shivers cascaded down my spine. Where did she go? Why did she touch my cross?

When we sat down, Trent's grandmother reached over and squeezed my arm. And Trent, true to his word, kept my hand in his and sat as close to me as possible. He was way too good for me, and I knew I should stop seeing him. But now that Abigail had called him her friend, I couldn't. I had to find out what she meant.

The mass was a series of readings, chants, and songs. Everyone sat, stood, and kneeled over and over. After about an hour and a half, the incense faded and the mass ended.

When we got out into the night, the cool air filled my lungs, the smell of the incense already a thing of the past. But Abigail's words haunted me. I needed to get to Farrell right away and tell him what had happened. Maybe he had answers.

WHEN I GOT HOME, I found the house almost completely dark. The only light came from a small lamp on the kitchen counter. Abigail had told me the journal was hidden, urged me to have faith and be strong, and then called Trent her friend. My hand went to my cross. I rubbed it between my thumb and forefinger. How did Abigail know Trent?

"Dominique."

With a gasp, I spun around to find Farrell standing by the kitchen fireplace, partly concealed in the shadows. My heart raced. "Farrell, you scared the crap out of me."

He walked closer to me, so close that our bodies almost touched.

"What happened?" he asked.

"I saw Abigail." Her delicate face and pure green eyes filled my head. "At church."

His brow furrowed. His peaceful eyes grew stormy.

Before he could say anything, I lifted my cross. "Look at this. Trent's grandmother gave it to me. She said it's been in her family for generations."

He eyed it curiously. "That's bloodstone."

I thought back to when Jan had emptied her bag of crystals and stones and told me to pick the one calling to me. "Jan showed me a rock like this. She said it's the stone of courage."

Farrell cradled the stone in his fingers. He closed his eyes. His white aura trickled out of his fingertips, wrapped around the cross, and pulsated against my chest. My heart beat so hard I wondered if he could hear it. He opened his eyes and released the cross.

"It's ancient," he said. "As old as man."

"This cross is that old?" My heart continued to race as the fear inside me grew.

"Yes," he said.

I recalled Trent's grandmother and her milky eyes and wrinkly hands. "She said it would remind me to have faith and be strong. It's the same thing that Abigail had said."

Farrell stood so close I could see my reflection in the fiery spark in his green eyes. I wanted him to get closer, wanted his body to press up against mine.

"And Abigail?" he asked.

"She touched my cross. Then her energy flowed into it and me and—"

Should I tell him what she had said about recognizing Trent and calling him her friend? Farrell was my Walker, assigned to protect me, but who would protect Trent? I couldn't have another death on my conscience, especially Trent's, and I knew if he got involved in my messed up life something would happen to him.

"What?" Farrell prodded.

Switching gears and ignoring anything that had to do with Trent, I said, "She said that Huxley did nothing wrong. She also told me my mom and dad had hidden Huxley's journal in the ocean by the tree."

He stepped away from me and ran his fingers through his hair. "In the ocean? By the tree? Does that mean anything to you?"

My mind ached from all the stress, my nerves shot and on edge. I twisted my hair. How could a tree and a book be in an ocean? It didn't make any sense. "No, it doesn't mean anything to me. But Farrell, we have to find it. Time is running out. I only have two days before I'm dead, and probably my parents, too."

He rubbed his temples. I wondered if I was as difficult to protect in my other lifetimes as I was in this one.

"Let's get some rest," Farrell said. "Maybe something will come to us by morning."

Anger and frustration mounted inside me. "What? Are you kidding? I could die in two days, and you want to sleep on it?"

"No, I don't want you to sleep on it, but it's almost three in the morning. You can't help if you're exhausted. I promise I'll do whatever I can to find the book, but you need to store up your energy." He held my chin and studied my face. "Dominique, I know you haven't slept in days. Please, you have to listen to me."

My tired eyes welled up with tears. "For so many weeks I've wanted all this to end, Farrell, wanted to die even. But now that everything is happening so fast and my parents have been captured, I want to live." Tears slipped out onto my face. "I'd give anything to have my parents back and go back to being normal."

Farrell wiped the tears from my face. He brought me in and held me tight. Even though it was our first hug, it didn't feel like it. I fit in his arms perfectly, my body relaxed and at ease against his. Without even thinking, I moved my hands up the back of his shirt and began rubbing them across his smooth and soft skin. He pulled me closer and whispered my name.

And then—I freaked. I yanked my hands out of his shirt and stepped away from him, horrified and embarrassed. "Farrell, I'm so sorry, I don't know why I did that."

His shoulders fell. He stepped away from me. "Don't worry about it. It's been a tough day. I'll see you in the morning." He couldn't get away from me fast enough.

BACK IN MY ROOM, I eagerly grabbed the snow globe Trent had given me. I ran my fingers across the cool glass while I studied the peaceful village. A perfectly shaped spruce tree stood in the middle. Behind it was a small white church with a tall steeple. To the right of that, was a cottage, and on the other side, a market. A winding cobblestone path joined the structures. I shook the globe and watched the snow fall on the tiny town.

"Wake up," I whispered. "It's snowing."

I kept my eyes fixed on the falling snow, thinking to myself that I was the one waking up.

CHAPTER *Twenty*

I AWOKE THE NEXT MORNING to a chill in my bones. I huddled under my covers, realizing a cold front must've blown in. The unpredictable Houston weather drove me crazy, and so did my messed-up life.

I didn't want to die… not anymore.

Today I needed to cut all ties to Trent. It wasn't fair to keep him hanging on. He deserved so much more than me. More importantly, he deserved to live.

I studied my palms. The cuts had closed and scabs had formed. They still ached, but not as much as before. And then I thought of Abigail—the way she had touched my cross, how she told me that my parents had hidden Huxley's journal in the ocean by the tree, and the way she looked at Trent.

None of it made sense.

I flung the covers off my bed and grabbed Trent's Rice sweatshirt from the stack of clothes on the chair. What were the odds of Trent having a Rice sweatshirt when suddenly Rice meant something more to me than just being a university in Houston?

My heart sped up. The coincidence had to mean something. Or was I over thinking everything? I called Infiniti.

"Hey, Infiniti," I said. "You doing okay?"

"I'm shitty." She let out a long sigh. "I'm stuck here with my mom, and she's trying to like hang with me or something. Thinks I need cheering up after all death in my life."

Guilt rippled through me. "It sounds like she's worried about you, Infiniti. You should give her a try, ya know? There's nothing wrong with a little cheer right now. I mean, it is Christmas after all."

"Dude, I'm Jewish," she said with a laugh.

I laughed back. "I'm sorry, I didn't know. Besides, you know what I mean."

"Yeah, I know. I'm just not used to all the hovering."

I'd give anything to have my mom bugging me, anything for her and my dad to be safe. "Hey, I borrowed a Rice sweatshirt from Trent. Is that where he's going to school next year?"

"You didn't hear? He got a full academic scholarship."

I gulped. "He did?"

"Yep, he's top of the class right now. *Numero uno.*"

The fact that he was going to Rice, the place where Julian Huxley taught, had to mean something. I hung up with Infiniti right away.

Trent, Abigail, Huxley and Rice were all connected. They had to be. But how? I slipped the sweatshirt over my white tank, put on some sweats, and tiptoed downstairs to the study so Farrell wouldn't hear me. I didn't want him to know that Trent linked to Abigail and Huxley because that would only jeopardize Trent, which was the last thing I wanted.

I opened the laptop and typed "Julian Huxley Biologist" and clicked to an image search.

The screen filled with black and white pictures. The first one was Huxley in his early twenties. Thin and well-groomed, he had short hair on the sides but a little puffy on top. He wore round, wire glasses and a three-piece suit. The second picture was him on the grass with what must've been his two kids on his lap. Another was him as a boy on the lap of his grandfather. There was even a picture of him as a young man all decked out in his army uniform. There were a few of him older, maybe in his sixties.

Finally, I came across a black and white picture of a group of people sitting on blankets having a picnic. I clicked the image and recognized the building in the background right away because I had seen it at the Rice campus. On one blanket sat Huxley and a young woman. The woman wore a white dress, white gloves, and a hat. On another blanket sat a Hispanic lady who wore a dark dress with a white apron with two kids on either side. I froze. My eyes studied the faces of the kids. My breathing stopped. It was Abigail, and a kid who looked exactly like Trent.

Farrell tapped on the doorframe. I slammed the laptop closed. My heart pounded. I tried to act normal.

"What are you doing?" he asked. He wore black sweatpants, and a tight white T- shirt. He leaned against the door.

"Nothing."

"Really?" He walked over and took my hand away from my hair, eyeing the laptop suspiciously.

"I, uh, just talked to Infiniti. She's having a rough day." I got up, and casually tucked the laptop under my arm. "I'm gonna go check on her. I won't be long."

"Dominique, I can't let you go."

Heat flushed my body. "I refuse to be a prisoner in my own house, Farrell. Okay? And with two days left to live, what can go wrong at this point?"

I hurried out of the room, went upstairs, quickly erased the search history on the laptop, then changed clothes. Farrell was trying to protect me, but I didn't care anymore. I needed to find out two things. First, who was that kid in the picture with Abigail? Second, how were Abigail and that kid connected to Trent?

While I didn't want to put Trent in danger, I needed to see him. Taking my mom's car would only make Farrell suspicious, but then I thought of Infiniti. She could take me to Trent's house. I folded the sweatshirt and tucked it under my arm. Returning the sweatshirt would be my excuse to bring up Rice.

My stomach tied in a giant knot as I walked to Infiniti's. When I passed Jan's, I saw a "For Sale" sign in her yard. I stopped, half-expecting her to ghostly image walk out, but it didn't.

"Sucks, doesn't it?"

I spun around. Infiniti was crossing the street to meet me. I exhaled, relieved to see her. "Yeah, it totally sucks."

We stared at the house. My face grew cold, and my nose started to run. "I need to see Trent real quick. Mind giving me a ride?"

"No problem. Come on."

Before we went into her house, she brought her finger to her lips and whispered, "My mom's taking a nap."

We tiptoed in, got her purse, and went out the back door to the garage. Getting into the car she said, "So, I need to tell you something."

She looked afraid, and I immediately thought something was wrong. "What is it?"

"I'm kinda seeing someone."

"Really? Who? And why didn't you tell me?"

She wrinkled her nose. "Dude, please don't think I'm awful. It just happened. I swear I didn't plan it."

I leaned against the car. "Infiniti, I have no idea what you're talking about."

She brought her hand to her mouth and started chewing her fingernails. "Don't judge me."

"Um, okay…"

She spit out what must've been a fingernail. "It's Billy. I'm seeing Billy Weber now." She cringed, waiting for my response.

I had never understood the attraction between Veronica and Billy. They were total opposites. But Infiniti and Billy? Now that made sense. They were so much alike: funny and easygoing.

It shouldn't matter that Veronica's death had brought them together. Why couldn't two people come together during a time of sorrow?

"I think it's great. He's a great guy, and you guys go really well together."

"Yeah?"

"Yeah. I even think Veronica would approve. After all, she was your friend. I'm sure she'd want you to be happy."

Her shoulders relaxed. "See? That's what I was thinking." She gave me a quick hug. "Thanks for being so cool."

Once in the car, she shoved three sticks of cinnamon gum in her mouth. "You think Trent will be home?"

Trent had said he'd be working all break, but since it was Christmas Day, I thought for sure he'd be home. "He should."

We wound our way out of my wooded neighborhood and into his. When we got to his house, I hesitated before getting out. What would I say to him? I ran my hand over the soft cotton sweatshirt.

"What gives?" Infiniti asked, smacking her gum.

Everything Trent had ever done for me filled my thoughts. The way he played with my hair and my fingers. The kiss at Infiniti's that he wouldn't remember because I had almost gotten him killed and Farrell had erased his memory. His tenderness at church when I had fainted. He needed to stay away from me—he and Infiniti both. After today, after I returned his sweatshirt and tried to find out about that picture, I would never see either one of them again. It was the only way to assure their safety.

"I need to move on, I guess. You know, start cutting ties before the end of the year when everybody goes their separate ways anyway."

Infiniti paused mid-chew. "Whoa, are you breaking up with him? On Christmas Day? That's beyond brutal."

I had never thought of us as being officially a couple, but I guess she did. Maybe everyone else, too. "Well, we're really not together. We're just friends."

Her eyes went wide, her mouth hung open, and her gum fell out and landed on her jeans. "For real?" She put her gum back in her mouth. "I mean, you're not believing your own bullshit, are you?"

I opened the car door. "I know what I'm doing." At least, I hoped I knew what I was doing. "Wait here, I'll only be a minute."

When I got to the front door, doubt flooded me. Infiniti was right, I couldn't do this. I turned to leave when the door opened.

"Hey!" Trent said, happy to see me. He wore tattered navy sweats, had his running shoes on, and held his phone in his hand. He pulled out his earbuds. "I wasn't expecting you."

"Sorry. I should've called before coming over. Were you heading out for a run?"

"Yeah, but it can wait. What's up?"

"Well, um, Infiniti brought me by so I could return this." I handed him the sweatshirt. "I didn't know you were going to Rice."

"Yep, it's a family tradition of sorts. My dad,

grandfather, and great grandfather all worked at Rice as groundskeepers. I'm breaking Avila tradition and going as a student."

That was it. The little boy in the picture with Abigail had to have been Trent's grandfather. I touched the cross at my neck and rubbed the stone between my fingers. His grandfather was Abigail's friend. It had to mean something, but what? It was almost as if Abigail was stalking me. First with Trent's grandfather, and then with Jan when she told Jan to move to Houston. Panic soared inside me.

"You wanna do something later?" he asked. "Maybe go to a movie?"

Nobody was safe around me, especially him. As much as I wanted to be with him, I knew I couldn't, not anymore. Even if it meant he'd hate me. "Trent, I'm going back North for college, and you're staying here. We should probably…" I shrugged my shoulders, trying to figure out what to say next. "…Stop hanging out."

He backed up. "Are you serious?"

I started to unclasp my necklace to give it back. "I'm sorry, Trent. But it's easier this way."

He held out his hand and stopped me. "Keep it." He tossed the sweatshirt at me. "This, too. And stay the hell away from me."

Shocked, I stood there while he jogged out of view. Tears filled my eyes. I dropped the sweatshirt on the porch and went back to Infiniti's car.

"He did not throw that sweatshirt in your face!" she said, chewing her gum fast. "Who the hell does he think he is?" She jerked the car in gear like she wanted to speed up and run him over.

I put my hand on her arm. "Infiniti, I deserved it. Let's go."

A huge lump formed in my throat. I hated myself for doing that to him, and he had every right to despise me.

Back home, I headed straight for my room, shut the door, and sat on the edge of my bed. I clutched my knees, my breathing rapid while my body trembled. My ocean-blue walls reminded me of Trent's eyes. I wanted to tear them down, wanted to erase all trace of him. And then I thought of the snow globe he had given me. I grabbed it, ready to smash it to bits, but instead rolled it under my bed and out of view.

I needed to calm down and pull myself together. The beach—thinking of the beach back home at Elk Rapids always relaxed me. I forced an image of the still blue water in my brain, but it wouldn't hold. Instead, my attention drifted to the tree outside my window—bare and stiff. Irritated, I brought my gaze back to my ocean-colored walls. Then I noticed the vent at the top of my ceiling right by the window.

"Farrell!"

He came in quick. I pointed to my walls. "My walls are the ocean." I pointed to my window. "And there is the tree." Lastly, I pointed to the vent.

Together we said, "In the ocean by the tree."

He brought a chair up against the wall, stood on it, and opened the vent. He stuck his arm in, patted around for a moment, when a look of discovery came over his face. He brought the book out.

"We've got it," he said.

All this time my parents had hidden the book right under my nose, here at home where my Walker protected me. And since he protected me, he also protected the book. My hands shook. Maybe I could really live. Maybe I didn't have to die after all.

Farrell and I sat on my bed. Before opening the journal, he set it down on my nightstand then looked me straight in the eye. "We go through this book together." His eyes narrowed a little. "No more secrets, Dominique. We don't have time for secrets."

Powerless, I could only control what nobody else knew. Right now, nobody knew about my feelings for Trent or his connection to Abigail and Huxley. I had to protect Trent at all cost. It was the least I could do after what I had done to him. Plus, I didn't know what, if anything, had happened between Farrell and me in our past lives. If there was something there, then I didn't want him to know how much Trent meant to me.

"No more secrets," I lied.

We opened the book. The water-stained ink smeared across the pages. We studied the letters, trying to make out the words. Between the two of us, we were able to figure out how Huxley met Abigail and discovered her powers.

In 1929, thirteen years after leaving his teaching position in Houston, Huxley met and fell in love with a young American girl while on a cruise. He left England and his wife and came back to the United States hoping to marry the girl and resume teaching at Rice. Neither happened. He did, however, receive permission to conduct studies at Rice.

"I roam the grounds, observing native Texan birds, insects, and just about any creature that will take my mind off my sorrow of losing the affection of my young, American love. For my sorrow is deep, and if I let it get away from me, I may not return from the depths of despair upon which I have found myself on many occasion."

"Farrell, Huxley was lovesick," I said. "Maybe even depressed." Suddenly I connected with Huxley because I too knew what it was like to want something I couldn't have.

The journal went on to describe the different animals he studied. After pages and pages of animal behavior, his writing became scribbled and hurried.

"This brown-haired boy and fair-haired girl of six years play every day in the quadrangle, sometimes supervised by the father of the boy who tends to the grounds. They are interesting to watch, and on this one occasion, when the boy fell from a tree, the girl rushed to his aid. With a touch to his chest, it appears she brought him back from death's door. But how? This I must discover, for in her there must be a power not yet identified."

I almost dropped the book. "Abigail saved—" I almost said Trent's grandfather, but stopped myself. "A boy. That's how Huxley discovered her abilities."

"It appears that way," Farrell said. "But what happened to Abigail?"

We read on. *"I have performed brain tests on the*

girl, which I called thinking games. The girl has correctly guessed every shape on the other side of each card I showed her. And the boy...he did not appear afraid at all, but stood close to her, almost like a protector of sorts. I must discover the secrets that lie within her brain and have heard of a new method to monitor electrical activity along the scalp. This method, called electroencephalography, or EEG, has been introduced by German physiologist and psychiatrist Hans Berger. Upon successful contact with Mr. Berger, I can use this machine to measure the voltage fluctuation resulting from ionic current flows within the neurons of her brain."

My body tensed. "Farrell, he was studying her brain."

Farrell's brow furrowed, but he remained quiet. I didn't want to read the rest because I knew it couldn't be good. But we had to know what happened to Abigail. We had to know the truth.

"I have successfully secured the use of an EEG machine and told the girl the machine would draw a picture of her brain activity. The boy attempted to dissuade the girl from participating, but she had nothing of it, proclaiming her desire to proceed."

"Farrell, she wanted to be tested," I whispered. Shivers crawled up and down my spine. My stomach twisted tight. The next few pages were smeared and illegible. We couldn't read the text again until ten pages later.

"This young girl is not of this world, but insists she is. Able to do what others are incapable of, transcending human abilities, she is unlike any human being I have encountered. If I can somehow study not only her brain waves but also the electrical impulses

that originate in her cortex, I should be able to discover the source of her power. If I can discover the source, I can understand it."

I gasped and covered my mouth. The source? What did that mean? And could it help me?

"The girl insisted I continue with my studies, that her energy source must be studied for the benefit of someone she calls the Marked One, someone not yet born unto this world. With great reluctance, I obey. Further, I believe her desires are having an unnatural influence on me for I fervently wish to cease with these tests, but am unable to do so."

Farrell put the book down. He looked deep into my eyes. "Dominique, take a breath."

I exhaled, not even realizing I had been holding my breath. "Farrell," my voice cracked. "The Marked One. They're talking about me."

"I know. And it appears Huxley didn't want to continue studying her, but Abigail made him." He squeezed my knee. "Can you continue?"

Every ounce of fear in me magnified. I didn't want to go on, but I knew I had to. "Yes."

"The girl instructed me to conduct electricity into her by delivering a current through her temples. As if robbed of all independent thought, I complied. When the blast entered her, something remarkable and altogether terrible happened. A blast of pink-hued light emitted from her rigid body. The light gathered at her fingers that clutched a black cross that hung around her neck, funneling into the religious object. I immediately ceased the current, but it was too late. She whispered to the crying boy at her side before handing him the cross. Then her body went limp."

Tears filled my eyes. My hand went to the

cross around my neck, the cross that Abigail had given Trent's grandfather that had now been passed on to me — the Marked One.

"Farrell," I whispered. "She died because of me."

CHAPTER
Twenty-one

My hands shook. My stomach tightened. Abigail wanted Huxley to study her, but why did she want him to kill her? Farrell and I flipped through the pages to read more, but the scribbled ink smeared all over and blended together.

Farrell slammed the book shut and chucked it at the wall. I stared at the worn leather cover and the yellowed paper that poked out. My hands went to my cross. I rubbed the warm smooth surface.

"I need to check something," Farrell said. White light trickled out of his hand and wrapped around his fingers. He touched the cross. My eyes fixed on his perfect face. White flecks the same color as his aura littered his pure green eyes, like tiny stars. His aura pulsed through the stone and into my skin, vibrating straight through my body. Warmth spread deep inside me and my head began to spin. He drew his hand away fast.

"What?" I asked. "What is it?"

"Her energy source is in there," he said. "I

didn't recognize it before, but I can tell now."

What? Her energy source hung from my neck? My skin prickled with fear. I swallowed hard while I recalled everything Farrell had told me about Transhumans. The only way we die is to get relocated, or absorbed by another energy source.

"She relocated her energy source," I muttered.

"Yes," Farrell said. "She put it in that stone." He ran his fingers through his hair and paced the room. "But why?" he asked, mostly to himself. "Especially if it can't be accessed."

"What do you mean, can't be accessed?"

He continued pacing while my anxiety soared. "When a Transhuman places their energy in an inanimate object, it's locked away forever."

Why would Abigail put her energy source in the cross if it couldn't help me? Finding it hard to breathe and feeling like the room was closing in on me, I excused myself to the bathroom and splashed water on my face. Water dripped down my chin while I stared at the reflection of the cross that hung from my neck. I was about to yank it off when Farrell knocked on the door.

"Dominique, are you okay?"

In two days I would face Tavion, the leader of the Tainted who wanted me dead. He had my parents. The cross that hung around my neck was useless. I jerked the door open. "No! I'm not okay!" I grabbed my necklace. "And this can't even help me."

"I might have something that can," he said.

Farrell went to his room and came back with a long black box. He opened the box and brought out two shiny, silver daggers. They were plain and slender with a fine tip.

"I'm not going to give you up, Dominique. When we face Tavion, you're going to kill him."

"What? Kill Tavion? Is it even possible?"

"There is power coursing through your veins," he said. "If you can touch Tavion with your blood, you might be able to kill him."

My mind raced. The image of Tavion's pale and gaunt face filled my mind. The last time I saw him I was on the brink of death, but managed to smear my blood on his face. It had burned his skin. But could my blood kill him?

I shook my head. "Farrell, I don't know. I mean, I know my blood burned his skin, but kill him?"

He lifted the daggers out of the box and handed them to me. They were cool and smooth, and surprisingly light.

"We let Tavion think we're turning you over in exchange for your parents," Farrell explained. "After the switch, you'll take one of these daggers, cut your palm, cover the metal with your blood, and plunge the weapon into him. Your blood must penetrate past his skin and go deep inside him. When it does, I think it can extinguish his energy source and kill him."

My hands had finally healed since my last encounter with Tavion when the sharp rocks I held had slashed my skin. Now I would have to cut them again, but this time on purpose. My palms throbbed. Every detail of the red desert flooded my senses. The heat filled my nose. The dirt invaded my lungs. I could even feel tiny granules of dirt under my fingernails.

"I thought a Transhuman couldn't die," I said. "That their energy source was either absorbed or transferred."

Farrell took the daggers out of my hands. "It is said that our energy source can be extinguished, like fire doused by water, though I've never heard of it happening before."

Every hair on my skin stood on edge. "Hold on," I said. "We're going to try something that's never been done before?"

"Yes," he said. "We are."

He placed the daggers in the box and leveled me with a serious look. "Get dressed and meet me downstairs. We have a lot of work to do."

I had no idea what he was up to, but I figured I should do what he said since this was it—my last days. If my Walker didn't have a plan, then I was completely screwed.

When I got downstairs, I found Farrell pacing the room, the daggers laid out on the coffee table. "When we show up for your surrender, you'll have your jeans tucked into your boots, one dagger in each. When Tavion releases your parents, I'll hand you over. When you get close enough, I want you to pull out one of the daggers, slash your palm, smear it with your blood, and stab Tavion in the chest."

I shuddered at the thought of getting close to Tavion. "I don't know if I can do it," I whispered.

"You have to do it," he said. "You have no choice, Dominique. This is it, your final life. Game over after this, for all of us. Got it?"

Farrell's words echoed in my head, the hard

tone in his voice vibrated in my ears. "You're right," I said. "I have no choice." I picked up the daggers, one in each hand. "Veronica and Jan died because of me. So did Abigail." Trent's bloodied face from our confrontation in the red desert flashed before my eyes. "I want nothing more than to kill Tavion for everything he's done."

"Good," Farrell said. "Let that anger fuel you. Now practice taking the dagger out of your boot and slashing your palm. You must be swift."

My hands throbbed. "You want me to cut myself right now?"

"No, you just need to practice the movements," Farrell said. "You need to get comfortable with the daggers. You need to maneuver them as if they're an extension of your body."

I placed one knife in each boot, the pointy end facing down. I walked around a little, trying to get used to them. Luckily, with my jeans tucked in, and with thick socks, it didn't feel so bad.

"Grab one of the daggers as quick as you can," Farrell said. "The other dagger will be your back up."

I exhaled, stood with my legs shoulder width apart, and tried to relax my hands while a million doubts raced through my mind. What if I couldn't grab the dagger fast enough? What if I dropped it and didn't have time to get the other? What if I couldn't cut my hand after all? And could I really plunge the dagger into Tavion's chest?

Farrell gave me a nod of encouragement that only heightened my anxiety because I didn't want to let him down. With my right hand, I went for the dagger on the inside of my left boot, but my hand caught on the top of the boot. I relaxed my hands again at my side. I went for the dagger again, but fumbled around inside my boot before bringing it out, and when I did, I dropped it.

"Not bad," Farrell said. "Now do it again, but with a firm grip."

"Farrell, thanks for the support and all, but that sucked."

"Keep trying," he said. "I know you can do it."

After over a few dozen tries, I managed to pull out the dagger and point it at my right palm, ready to slice my skin.

"That was good," Farrell said. "Now keep practicing until you're faster. Tavion can't know what you're doing until it's too late."

The day turned to night as I continued pulling the dagger from my boot. My hands ached. My arms grew sore. I was beginning to think I could never do it fast enough. Frustration escalated inside me, and I was about to throw the dagger at the wall as hard as I could when Farrell appeared right beside me, his hand on my arm.

"I know it's not easy," he said. His eyes locked on mine while he pried the dagger from my grip. "Let's take a quick break."

Tears flooded my eyes, and I swallowed the lump that had lodged in my throat. "Okay."

After pulling myself together and having a quick bite that I forced down, we were back at it. I pulled the stupid dagger out of my boot over and over while Farrell urged me to be faster. Just when I was about to quit, I pulled the dagger out and pointed the tip at my palm in one swift motion.

"I did it!" I slid the dagger back in my boot and tried it a few more times to make sure I had it down, and I did.

"Good. Now let's do your left hand in case you can't use your right," Farrell instructed.

Can't use my right hand? My body trembled. My throat tightened as I imagined all the things Tavion could do to my right hand: tie it up with his aura, burn it to bits, cut it off. I tried to shut off my imagination, but had a hard time.

"You shouldn't have said that," I said.

"I'm sorry," he said. "But we need to be ready for anything."

Farrell was right; I needed to be able to pull out the dagger with my left hand in case something happened. Since I wasn't left-handed, taking the dagger out of my right boot and positioning it at my right palm took forever. My weak and clumsy left hand was hard to control, and almost every time I pulled the knife out, I dropped it. But I couldn't quit, so I kept at it even though my arm started to burn and my hand started to tingle.

With a jerk, I brought the dagger out and brought it to my hand, but my movement was too heavy. The dagger plunged straight through my palm. Pain shot through me. Blood gushed all over.

Farrell zipped over to me and took my hand. His aura trickled out of his fingers and gathered at my palm. My head swooned. My body swayed. His light sent the blood back into my hand. My cut closed. Farrell held me tight, lifted me, and set me on the couch.

Sadness and despair flooded me, and fear—

fear that I'd never see my parents again, that I wouldn't be able to kill Tavion, that I'd be murdered... again.

"You should rest," Farrell said. "We face Tavion tomorrow at midnight, and we need to be ready."

"No!" I struggled to get up. "I need to keep practicing!" Farrell held me down with a firm grip. "Let me go!"

A white mist circled his fingers as he touched my forehead. "Close your eyes, Dominique. Rest."

Warmth filled my body while I fought to keep my eyes open. I counted the tiny white flecks in Farrell's eyes, trying to stay awake, but I couldn't hold on. Instead, I drifted into a deep, dark, and restless sleep.

CHAPTER
Twenty-two

Wake up, I said to myself over and over in my head. My bones were heavy and stiff. My body jerked with the sensation of falling. Finally, my eyes flew open. I wasn't on the couch anymore. Instead, I found myself standing in a dark place. The musty odor of earth and dirt surrounded me. My heart pounded. I groped around in front of me and tried to get my bearings.

"Dominique," a voice whispered.

My eyes and ears strained. My body covered in shivers. "Who's there?"

A small beam of white light appeared in front of me and slowly grew bigger. I shielded my face, afraid of what it might be, every muscle ready for an attack.

"Dominique."

I lowered my hands and found myself in front of my mom and dad! We were in a cave-like area, or a shed of some sort. I couldn't tell. I grabbed my mom, hugged her tight, and buried my face in her shoulder. A trace of her floral perfume filled my senses.

"Oh, Dominique," she said, stroking my hair. "We've been trying for days to reach you."

Dad came up behind me and wrapped his arms around both of us. Here, in between them, I finally felt safe. Tears slid down my cheeks. "Is this real?" I asked. "Am I really here with you?"

Mom and Dad released me. Mom wiped the tears from my cheeks. "Yes," she said. "This is real."

I studied their battered and bruised faces. "What has he done to you?"

"Don't worry about us," Dad said. "We're fine. But Dominique, you must listen carefully. There's not much time." He placed his hands on my shoulders. "You and Farrell need to know that Tavion—"

A crash of thunder boomed in my ear, vibrated straight through my body, and shook the ground beneath my feet. Mom and Dad vanished, in their place swirled a column of gray vapor. It stretched at least ten feet high and five feet wide as it whipped around in front of me like a tornado. Out stepped the Tracker who had found me at the Rice campus, the same Tracker who later told me that Tavion had my parents and asked for my surrender, the Tracker who looked like Farrell except he had black hair, not blond.

"Sorry to break up your family reunion," the Tracker said.

My pulse raced. My heart quickened. "What do you want?"

"Want?" He got closer. "Some alone time with you before your death, that's all."

He tilted his head to the side, and studied me. "Do you remember anything?" My mind raced, wondering why he would ask me that. "Did your Walker tell you about me?" he went on. "About who I am?"

I continued backing up until I bumped into a wall. Bits of rock landed on my shoulders. What was he talking about?

"So, he hasn't. Allow me to formally introduce myself." He bowed. "My name is Fleet. Farrell and I are very close. We go way back."

My mind shouted for Farrell. In a flash, white lightening crackled through the air. Farrell appeared, his hands on Fleet's neck, choking him while his white aura trickled out of his fingers. Farrell flung Fleet away from me, and Fleet crashed onto the floor. Farrell grabbed my hand and pulled me close as Fleet got to his feet and dusted off his pants.

"Walker, you know that's not fair. Trackers can't use force against fellow Transhumans after a surrender. But I guess you never were one to follow the rules, were you?"

Never one to follow the rules? My mind raced. Panic soared through my veins. How much did I really know about Farrell?

"You are the one breaking the rules of surrender, Fleet. Not me."

"Me? Break the rules? Never!" Fleet said. "You should know that about me. Ask the Marked One yourself. I never laid a hand on her. Isn't that right, Marked One?"

I stayed silent.

"We are leaving," Farrell said. "Stand back."

Fleet kept his glare on Farrell before he smiled and stepped away. He crossed his arms and stared at us while Farrell transported us away through the mist that had trickled out of his hand and gathered at our feet.

We landed back home on the couch, Farrell on top of me. He got up quick. "Are you okay?"

Fleet's words repeated in my head. *Farrell and I are very close. Never one to follow the rules.*

"I'm fine," I answered.

The dark sky had turned a light shade of gray. I must've been asleep for hours but it felt like only a few minutes.

"It's almost morning," Farrell said. "You should go back to sleep. You need as much rest as possible."

Go back to sleep? After everything Fleet had said? I grabbed Farrell's arm. "You owe me an explanation."

"Dominique, do you trust me?"

Trust him? My parents had summoned him to protect me for nine lifetimes now. They wouldn't have done that if he couldn't be trusted. But everything Fleet had said raced through my mind. I didn't want to doubt Farrell, but I couldn't help myself. "Fleet said you and he went way back, and that you didn't follow the rules. What did he mean?"

Farrell ran his fingers through his hair. "Tavion can never be trusted. Neither can his Tracker or anyone affiliated with him. They're liars, Dominique. And they'll do anything to win this war. The only thing we can do is be as prepared as possible. Our fates will be determined tonight at midnight."

As much as I wanted to believe him, a part of me stayed skeptical. But he was all I had, and I needed him. "I believe you," I whispered. I thought of my parents. "Farrell, I saw my parents. They had a warning about Tavion but couldn't tell me because they vanished when Fleet appeared. But whatever it was, it was big. Big enough for them to summon me."

Farrell continued pacing as he considered my words. "We have to be ready. At this point, that's all we can do."

The gray sky outside had grown lighter. There was no way I could sleep anymore. My mind had overloaded. My nerves completely frazzled. Instead, Farrell and I spent the day preparing for our midnight confrontation with Tavion.

I practiced with the daggers for hours. I was still a little shaky with my left hand, but as the day faded back into night again, I finally got it. Quick and with both hands, I could whip out the daggers and place them at my palms. Over and over, with speed and precision, I had mastered the movement. I hoped I could do it later when it counted.

At around ten, we stopped. Farrell handed me a bottle of water. "We need to talk about where we want to meet Tavion."

Water dribbled out of my mouth. I wiped it away. "We get to decide?"

"Yes," Farrell said. "That was one of my conditions of our surrender, don't you remember?"

I thought back to that night at the campus when Fleet had appeared. He showed me my parents, and then asked for my surrender. Farrell's words came back to me. "Tell Tavion we'll be ready for surrender in three days at the place of our choosing when the moon is at its peak."

"The place of our choosing," I muttered.

Immediately I thought of the beach. It always calmed me. If I was going to confront someone who wanted me dead, someone who had killed me in my prior lives, I wanted it to happen there. For some reason I thought I'd have a chance at the beach. Maybe there I wouldn't die. Plus, I had never seen the ocean and this might be my only opportunity. I had to take it.

"Galveston Island," I said.

Farrell hesitated for a second. "Galveston it is."

"How will Tavion know the place?" I asked.

"Once you issued your surrender, he locked on your energy source," Farrell explained. "He's been following you this whole time and will appear wherever we are."

I imagined Tavion hovering over my house following my every move. There was no way to escape him, only to defeat him. I went upstairs to get ready. The night was cool, in the low fifties, and it was sure to be cooler on the island. My stomach stayed tight, my nerves elevated while I slipped on a long-sleeved black shirt and a black sweater. When I stood in front of the mirror to pull my hair up in a ponytail, I stopped because I hardly recognized myself. My pale face and sunken cheekbones reminded me of Tavion.

Who had I become?

My phone beeped, interrupting my train

of thought. It was a text from Trent with two words — I'm sorry — the same two words he had texted me over and over all day. It was better for him if I didn't respond, better for both of us. I got on my hands and knees and brought the snow globe out from under my bed where I had tossed it earlier. I held the round glass in my hands, shook it, and watched the snow come down.

Sorrow and despair descended on me while I studied the tiny town. If only I could go back home to Michigan, make all of this go away, and be normal again. But there was no way.

I put the globe back on my nightstand. Would I ever see this room again? Or this house? I had no idea, but I would find out soon enough.

CHAPTER
Twenty-three

MY HEAD POUNDED, MY TIRED eyes hurt, and my body ached as we drove to Galveston. And my mind—it flooded with worries, doubts, and regrets. I didn't know if I could kill Tavion. Would I be strong enough? Would Farrell's plan work? And what about Fleet and what he had said about Farrell? I wanted to trust Farrell, but something didn't feel right. I sensed he was keeping something from me.

And then I kept thinking of the shock and confusion on Trent's face when I handed him his sweatshirt and told him we should stop hanging out. He would never know that I didn't mean it. Besides, if I had told him the truth, what good would it have done if I was going to die anyway? That would only make things worse.

Death… I needed to stop thinking about dying. If I had any chance of winning, I needed to change my thoughts, no matter how hard.

I clutched the bloodstone cross that hung around my neck. If it couldn't help me defeat

Tavion, then maybe it served another purpose. When Trent's grandmother gave it to me, she said to have faith and be strong. Abigail had said the same thing when she had touched it at Christmas Eve mass. But what about the fact that Abigail held it when she died and then gave it to Trent's grandfather? Did it mean anything? Or maybe the cross simply served as a reminder to believe in myself and not give up?

"Do you want to tell me what you're thinking?" Farrell asked.

"No," I said. "I don't."

I crisscrossed my arms over my stomach, angled my body toward the car door, and stared out the window at the full moon that filled the sky. The last thing I wanted to do was talk.

The busy Houston traffic and bright lights faded to a quiet road surrounded by fields. Even the stars popped out now that we were out of the big city. After about an hour, we arrived in Galveston. The town was small, flat, and quiet. The roads were empty. My stomach twisted so tight I needed to go to the bathroom. I spotted a gas station.

"Can you pull over up there? I need to go to the restroom."

Farrell rolled into a parking spot on the side of the station away from the street.

"I'll be right back," I muttered.

The bathroom reeked like dirt and piss. The white walls were covered in graffiti. My stomach heaved, and I barely made it to the stall in time to barf out what little food I had inside me. After my stomach emptied, it spasmed and lurched for a while trying to find more to push out, but there was nothing left.

I grabbed some toilet paper, wiped my mouth, stepped out of the stall, and saw Colleen — the Transhuman disguised as my homeroom teacher, a Pure who was on my side. I dropped my tissue. How did she get here?

"Ms. Ryken, I mean, um, Colleen, I didn't hear you come in."

She wore the same outfit she always had on. Black pants, tall black boots, a long black jacket with a white camisole. But she didn't have the white staff I had seen her hold the night that Farrell, Trent, and I transported out of the red desert and into my den at home.

"I didn't want to startle you," she explained.

Her gaze zeroed in on my cross. My hand covered my necklace, and I backed away a little. "When you left, you said you were going to search for my mom and dad."

She stepped closer, ignoring my question. "Dominique, may I see your cross?"

My heart raced. Why did she want to see my cross? I continued backing away, my mind shouting for Farrell. In a flash, he burst through the door. Colleen raised her hand, directing a stream of gray mist at Farrell. Her blast sent him flying through the wall, out of the bathroom, and into the parking lot. He landed with a thud, smoke rising from his body.

Colleen lowered her hand, looked at me, tilted her head, and smiled. Her body blurred into a misty haze, turned into Veronica, Jan, Abigail and then Julian Huxley before taking on the shape of

Fleet. "Did you know that Trackers can change their appearance? It's one of our special talents."

Farrell remained motionless out on the pavement outside while Fleet and I faced off in the half-destroyed bathroom. I remembered the daggers were still in the car. It was me and Fleet, and I was defenseless.

A store attendant burst into the bathroom. Fleet shot out a stream of energy, and the guy froze in place like a mannequin. Police sirens wailed in the distance.

"Dominique, I promise I won't hurt you," Fleet said in a low voice. "All I want is your cross, and then I'll let you and your Walker continue on to the beach for your big surrender."

I wrapped my hand around the stone. I needed to stall Fleet and give Farrell a chance to recover from the blast. Or maybe the cops would get here soon, though Fleet would probably immobilize them, too. Either way, I needed time.

"Farrell wouldn't tell me who you are," I blurted out. Fleet froze in place, and a hint of sadness flashed across his face. "And I want to know. Will you tell me?"

I studied his movements while he considered my request. He ran his fingers through his dark hair. He tilted his head to the side. He was tall and slender and perfectly chiseled. I gasped. "You and Farrell are—"

"Brothers," Farrell said from the blasted opening of the brick wall. His clothes were singed, his face smeared with ash. He gathered up a ball of white energy and held it in his hand. "Back away, Fleet."

Fleet backed away from me. The police sirens sounded closer.

"Dominique," Farrell said. "Walk over to me."

"You're not gonna win, Farrell. You never have, and you never will," Fleet said.

Farrell held my hand as I climbed out of the blown opening and over crumbled brick. He shoved the car keys in my hand. "Start the car," he whispered.

I ran to the car and fired up the engine. Farrell backed away from the gas station, eyes on Fleet, his weapon still gathered in his palm. I could see Fleet saying something to Farrell, but Farrell wasn't responding. When Farrell got to the car, he hurled his energy at Fleet. It shot out like a lightning bolt.

He jerked open the passenger side door and hopped in. "Drive! Now!"

I slammed the car in reverse and tore out of there. My heart beat wildly while a wave of terror hit me. Farrell's brother was on the other side.

"What the hell, Farrell! Why didn't you tell me who he was?" I slapped my hands against the steering wheel. "You should've told me!"

"Turn here," he ordered. His jaw clenched, his hands curled up into fists at his lap, his white mist still pulsing around his fingers.

"Farrell! That was your brother!"

"Fleet stopped being my brother the minute he picked the wrong side," Farrell spat out. "Now he is a Tracker, nothing more."

The dark road commanded my attention, so for now, I laid off the questions. We drove down a street that ran parallel to a vast darkness that had to be the ocean. The full moon overhead illuminated a portion of the choppy waves, but everything to the right and left was black. Not even the full moon could light up the entire ocean, it was that massive.

We drove until we got far enough from civilization that the only lights on the road were ours. Farrell directed me to an empty parking lot adjacent to white beach dunes. After parking, he grabbed the box of daggers from the back seat, got out of the car, and started walking to a narrow path that led up and over the dunes. Instead of following him, I leaned against the car and crossed my arms.

"I'm not coming!" I called out. The cold and powerful wind whipped across my face, forcing me to inhale the salty air. Farrell paused midstride. "I'm not taking another step until you tell me everything. And if you don't, I'm not gonna fight. I'm just gonna let Tavion take me."

Farrell came back to me. He studied my face and lowered his shoulders. "I'll tell you everything. But first, let me show you the ocean."

We walked over the dunes and to the beach. My boots sank into the soft sand. As we neared the surf, the sand became more compact with each step. I took in the scene in front of me. The enormity of the sight took my breath away. The roaring surf filled my ears while white capped waves rushed to the shore. Sprays of saltwater sprinkled my face. The large circular moon cast a soft white glow straight down the middle of the enormous and wild Gulf of Mexico, the gateway to the Atlantic Ocean.

Back home, the Elk Rapids Beach would be partially frozen, still and quiet. Here it was wild and raw—like my emotions and my life these past few months. The gulf also reminded me of Farrell—so calm and peaceful at times, and at others so strong and fierce.

"Amazing, isn't it?" Farrell asked.

"It's incredible."

He opened the box and handed me the daggers. "Put these in your boots, and I'll tell you everything."

Shivers ran down my spine. I couldn't tell if they were from the cool metal or my fear. I slipped the daggers in place and then spotted a white feather sticking out of the sand right by me. I took it. As soon as I did, the violent ocean waves stilled, the wind stopped, and the beach transformed from Galveston to Elk Rapids Beach. Only the moon-filled sky and the stars-littered heavens remained the same.

"Remember I told you to come here when you're scared?" Farrell asked.

"Yes, I remember."

Farrell opened his hand. White mist trickled out, forming into a long white feather while the one in my hands disappeared. "This feather has always brought you here because I left it for you," he said.

"What do you mean you left it for me?"

"I left it in your memory, so you would have something to hold on to from your past."

I didn't know what to say, had no idea what he was talking about.

Farrell handed the feather to me. He looked

up at the sky. "I remember it like it was yesterday, even though it was lifetimes ago. We were sitting right here, at this very spot, staring out at the bay. It was me and you and we were saying our good-byes because we didn't know if we would ever see each other again, if we would even be alive after facing Tavion." He glanced out at the water and then back at me, waiting for a response but I had none. I was speechless.

"When we got up to leave, you found a white feather on the sand. You said it was the same color as hope, that it was a sign that we would make it, that we would defeat Tavion and find each other. Well, you were partly right. While we never defeated Tavion, we did find each other, over and over, lifetime after lifetime."

Again, I said nothing.

"But every time we found each other, you remembered less and less." Farrell stroked the white feather that rested on my palm. "Your parents and I hoped that in this life you might remember something, but you didn't. And then we figured we could use that to our advantage—make all new choices since nothing we had done so far had worked."

My mind raced, my skin tingled, my heart pounded against my chest. Was he telling me that my memory kept diminishing in each life until finally I remembered nothing at all?

"Dominique, say something."

My hands shook. My eyes watered. I couldn't look at him. "You remember everything? You and my parents? I'm the only one who doesn't?"

He moved closer to me. "Yes."

Fear filled me, followed by betrayal and then anger. Clutching the feather, I pounded my fists against his chest. "This whole time I thought I was crazy! And you guys didn't tell me! How could you do this to me?"

He held my wrists. "We thought it was the best thing. You have to believe me, Dominique. Everything we've ever done has been to protect you."

I knew he was telling me the truth, but I couldn't calm down, I was too pissed. And then the reality of what he had said sunk in. This whole time I kept thinking that if we knew what had happened in the past, it would help. But they did know, and it wasn't helping. "In each life, you guys remembered what had happened before, but you still couldn't save me. Why would this life be any different?"

Farrell didn't answer.

"Tell me," I said. "I want to know."

"There's a lot different in this life." He paced the sand. "Remember I said we were all on our ninth life? That all those linked to you have been waging this war now nine times?"

"Yes."

"There are two who are new. Two on their first life who have become strongly connected to you."

I remembered when Jan told me about soul lives. I was a nine, Infiniti a one. "Infiniti," I said.

"Yes. And there's one other."

He didn't have to say it. I knew exactly who he was talking about. "Trent."

He continued to pace. "Yes, Trent."

My body trembled. I grabbed my necklace.

"Can this cross help? Did Trent's grandmother give it to me for a reason?"

"I don't know. And we've run out of time."

I sank to my knees. Was this life, my last life, destined to end like all the others? And what about Infiniti and Trent? Did getting mixed up with me seal their fate somehow?

"Will they be okay? Infiniti and Trent? I mean, I can't be responsible for anyone else's death, I can't."

"As far as I can tell, they'll be all right." Farrell stared at the sky for a second before kneeling in front of me. "Dominique, it's almost midnight." He reached out to touch my face, but dropped his hand. "There's something else you need to know."

I bit the inside of my cheek, desperately trying to remain calm. My back stiffened as I braced myself for whatever Farrell was about to say.

"When Fleet said I was breaking the rules, he was right. You see, Walkers are responsible for protection only. We're not supposed to become involved with our charge." He inched closer to me. Pain etched across his face. "We're not supposed to form... relationships." He took my hands. "Dominique, in each life we—"

"Fall in love," I muttered.

Everything made sense now. The faded memories of him that bubbled to the surface, our instant connection, the feeling of safety when I was near him—it was because we had been in love not once, but eight times. Shock rippled through me. All the times I thought I had known him were real. It wasn't in my head.

"Dominique, I love you." He squeezed my

hands. "I have always loved you. Now and forever. With everything that I am."

Tears trickled down my cheeks. He wiped them away and stared into my eyes. Like magnets, our bodies came together. Our lips touched. A blast of recognition shot through me. My body shuddered. A familiar and passionate longing for him grew in the pit of my stomach and spread throughout me as I finally remembered my love for him.

He pulled away from me and held my face. "I'm so sorry I didn't tell you sooner."

Before I could say anything, a crashing sound reverberated all around me, ringing so forcefully my teeth chattered. The calm and peaceful beach faded back to the choppy and violent waves of the Gulf Coast.

"It's time," Farrell said. He got to his feet and helped me up. He stood in front of me, feet planted wide, hands formed into fists. "Be ready."

CHAPTER
Twenty-four

I HAD SPENT THE LAST month not knowing if I was crazy or sane, if Farrell meant something to me or not. Now that I had all the answers, I was still going to die… unless I could kill Tavion.

The Gulf wind slapped my face and flipped my ponytail back and forth. The daggers in my boots pressed up against my ankles. I curled my hands into balls to keep my fingertips warm. I needed them ready to grasp the hilt of the knives and pull them out of my boot. Everything was up to me now.

"He's coming," Farrell said.

My fists tightened even more. My fingernails dug into my skin. The glow from the moonlight revealed a dark and hazy mass out in the ocean. It hovered over the waves and approached in slow motion. I narrowed my eyes and made out the form of Tavion. I also noticed the landscape behind him was changing. The dark ocean and white-capped waves were transforming into red rock and dirt. With a gasp, I realized he was taking away my ocean and replacing it with his red desert. With each of Tavion's steps, the desert grew until it overcame every wave and ripple. The saltwater sprays and moisture in the air became oven-like heat as the water and sand turned to red dirt.

My mind replayed everything that had happened to me back at the red desert when Tavion had almost killed me. My palms throbbed where the rocks had gashed my palms. The birthmark at the back of my neck pulsed. My throat closed as if Tavion was strangling me all over again. I forced myself to calm down and redirected my mind to the image of the beach, hoping it would give me strength, but it didn't. I was scared as hell.

Tavion's tall and bone-thin frame glided closer until he stopped ten feet in front of me. His laser-like gaze glued on me, his brow furrowed, his pale, and gaunt face stuck in an angry glare.

"I'm here for the Marked One."

Farrell stepped in front of me, breaking Tavion's line of sight. "She's ready for surrender. But first, you must release Caris and Stone."

Hopeful anticipation filled me at the thought of being reunited with my parents. With them freed, and Farrell by my side, it would be four against one. Maybe my last life would break my death cycle.

"I will release them as agreed, Walker," Tavion said.

Gray mist trickled out of Tavion's hand until it formed a thin rectangular mass. It was exactly like the mass Fleet had made when he had asked for my surrender at Rice.

"Open your eyes," a voice whispered at my ear. I spun around, looking for the source, but didn't see anyone.

"I'm right here," the voice said again.

Abigail shimmered into view beside me. I stared at Tavion to see if he noticed her, but he gave no indication. "Only you can see me." She looked at Tavion and then back at me. "Now do as I say. Open your eyes. See what's before you. Feel what is happening."

The gray mist that came from Tavion formed a doorway. My parents stood on the other side in their dark prison. But what exactly did Abigail want me to see? I started to ask her, but she had vanished.

"Step forward," Tavion said to my parents.

They stepped through the thin gray mist, and walked to Farrell. Relief should've flooded me, but it didn't. I was missing something, but I couldn't figure out what.

See what's before you. Feel what is happening.

I studied each unfolding detail—the gray mist that came from Tavion, my parents walking out of the mystical opening. But what was wrong? This was what we wanted, right?

Farrell hid his hands behind his back, his white, crackling energy building around his fingers. Mom and Dad filed in beside him. Standing alongside Farrell, they kept their hands behind their backs, too. Energy gathered around their fingers, just like Farrell. The three of them were about to attack. Was that it? Was that what Abigail wanted me to see?

See what's before you. Feel what is happening.

Farrell shifted his stance a little. Mom and Dad's energy continued to build. Tavion remained motionless, no doubt waiting for me to come forward, when he ran his bony fingers through his white hair. And that's when I figured it out. Fleet ran his fingers through his hair, just like Farrell, and could change shapes. And his mist—it was gray while Tavion's was black.

"It's a trick! That's not—!"

Mom, Dad, and Farrell blasted their energy at Tavion. Streaks of light exploded in the air—white from Farrell, gold from my mom, and silver from my dad. Their auras crackled through the air and penetrated straight through Tavion's body. The odor of sulfur and metal filled my nose and clogged my throat. Tavion's body shook until an array of gray electricity shot out of his body and flooded the red heat-filled sky. Once the gray blast ceased and all the energy had emptied from his body, Tavion toppled to the ground with a thud.

I caught my breath and held it, waiting to see if the person they had killed was Fleet like I thought, hoping I was wrong and that it was really Tavion. Mom wrapped her arms around me. Farrell and Dad approached the body with caution. As they neared, the white hair faded to black, the hollow cheeks filled out. Tavion disappeared and in his place laid Fleet—dead.

"No!" Farrell hollered. His voice echoed all around me, filling every space of the empty and hot desert air. He fell to his knees at his brother's side.

"Sorry I'm late," a deep and raspy voice said.

It sent the mark at the nape of my neck ablaze with pain. My knees buckled. If not for my mom, I would've fallen. Tavion appeared on the other side of Fleet. His face covered in a sick grin. His body pulsed with black streaked electrical blasts.

"You did this to him!" Farrell hollered.

"No, I didn't," Tavion said. "You three did. And for that, I am eternally grateful. He was of no more use to me."

Sweat trickled down my back and chest. My fear rose to an all-time high.

Mom held my arm. "Run when I let go," she whispered in my ear.

I gave a slight nod, but had no intention of running. I was going to push through my fear and fight. After all, that was the plan—slash my palm and attack Tavion after he released my parents. Now that they were free, it was up to me. I quickly peeled my sweater away, thinking I'd have more mobility with just my black tank underneath.

"Run!" Mom called out.

She released me, but instead of running away, I charged for Tavion. Before I made it to him, Mom, Dad, and Farrell blasted their energy at him. The heat and power from their attack knocked me down, and I fell on my back. The pointy daggers poked through my socks and dug into my skin, right above my ankles. I could feel blood ooze under my foot.

Shifting the daggers so I could get up, I noticed that Mom, Dad and Farrell's blasts had stopped right in front of Tavion and trickled into his hands. That couldn't be good.

Crouched and ready to finish my charge, I started to go for my daggers. Before I could complete my action, Tavion hurled the halted mass of energy back at Farrell and my parents. An explosion of light erupted. When the phenomenon faded, I saw Farrell and my parents on the ground, motionless. A black mist hovered over them and pressed them to the ground like a weight. Tavion had encased them in his blast. But were they alive?

Tavion sauntered over me to me, towering over me like a supernatural devil. "I really like you, more than any other you before."

Anger filled me. "Well, I hate you."

My ankles throbbed. Blood pooled at the bottom of my feet. A thick black vapor extended from Tavion's arms. The stream wrapped around my torso like a slithering snake, gripped my body, and lifted me into the air. My feet dangled while I hovered face to face with him.

"What to do now?" Tavion taunted with a click of his tongue.

Between clenched teeth, I managed to say, "Now I kill you."

Tavion let out a growling laugh. It started out low and grew until my ear drums vibrated. I extended my arms, but couldn't reach my boots. I needed him to drop me.

"Put me down, you coward!" I kicked him with my legs, not caring anymore about my blood-soaked feet. "Or are you that afraid of me?"

Tavion's eyes narrowed. He brought my face close to his. Heat escaped his thin lips and brushed against my skin while the metallic odor of blood assaulted me.

"I'm going to enjoy this," Tavion snarled. "Let's see what you got."

He dropped me. I went for the dagger in my right boot and brought it out quick, but arm froze mid-motion. Heat wrapped around my skin and penetrated straight to my bone. The dagger turned bright red and burned my flesh. With a yell, I pried my fingers open and let it fall from my hand.

"Oh, my," Tavion said between curled lips. "I've gone and spoiled your heroic attack, haven't I?"

What? He knew about the daggers? Was that what my parents were trying to warn me about when they had appeared in my dream? That somehow Tavion had discovered our plan?

"Now it's my turn to kill you," Tavion said. "Once and for all."

I stared him down, raised my chin, and readied for his attack, but it didn't come. Instead, he cast out another stream of rectangular shaped vapor like earlier. My stomach tightened, my heart galloped while a figure formed.

"But first, I want you to hurt like never before, Marked One. Before I kill you, I will slaughter every person you love, beginning with this one."

The mist faded. My mouth fell open. It was Trent. He ran straight for me.

"Dominique!"

"No! Trent! Go back!"

"Too late for that," Tavion said with a smile.

Before Trent made it to me, Tavion lifted him in the air with a blast of energy and held him there. I went for my other dagger and ran for Tavion, but he stopped me and lifted me up next to Trent. The dagger burned inside my hand and fell from my clutches.

"What the hell!" Trent kicked and punched mid-air, trying to break loose from Tavion's hold, but the clad-tight vapor held him firm.

I grabbed my cross and held it tight. Trent's grandmother and Abigail had said to have faith and be strong. But right now, I had neither. Pain attacked every inch of my body. Dark splotches littered my sight. The red desert moved up and down.

Don't pass out, not now.

"Dominique, hold on!" Farrell called out. He and my parents were on their feet but still held captive in Tavion's dome-like mist of energy. They blasted their own energy, trying to escape Tavion's trap, but they couldn't break through.

"Trent, I'm so sorry," I called out.

Trent's body stilled, his blue eyes landed on me. "Dominique, whatever is happening is not your fault."

I wanted to believe him, wanted to rid myself of the immense guilt I carried for causing the deaths of so many people, but I couldn't... unless I could somehow save him, Farrell, and my parents. I had no idea if it was possible, but I had to try.

"You are so pathetic, Tavion!" I spat out. "You used Fleet to do your dirty work, and then killed him! Only a total loser would do that!"

A growl escaped Tavion's lips.

"And now you want to kill everyone before you kill me because you're desperate for what, vengeance? Vengeance against a seven-teen-year-old girl you've already killed eight times? I mean, who the hell really cares!"

Mist and heat wrapped tight around my chest.

"You probably don't even want to kill me, you sick bastard, and you're just putting on this big show for everyone! I mean, what would you do without me? What purpose would you even serve if I weren't alive? Huh? You're nothing without me!"

Pain shot through my birthmark and explod-ed through my body. I gritted my teeth. "Let's face it, Tavion. You! Need! Me!"

Trent plummeted to the ground. The misty vapor surrounding Farrell and my parents col-lapsed. Like a freight train crashing into me, Tav-ion blasted every molecule of his energy my way. It filled me up, ripping me high into the air. My limbs went stiff. My body almost tore apart. My head flung back. The red sky burst with white light before going black.

WHEN I OPENED MY EYES, I was back at Elk Rapids Beach. Abigail and Jan were in front of me. Jan radiated peace and happiness. The worry lines around her eyes and mouth were smoothed out. Abigail looked happy, too, with an innocent smile on her delicate face. She wore the white dress that I had seen at church, but this time it was tied up at her knees like she had been running up and down the shore.

They had found each other.

"What… happened?" I patted my chest. Where… am… I?"

"Your soul is in the space between," Abigail said. "But your body is still over there."

She pointed over my shoulder. When I looked, I saw the red desert. My body sprawled out on the floor. My limbs looked crooked and twisted. My eyes were wide open. Blood dripped out of my mouth. Mom, Dad and Farrell blasted their energy at Tavion. He hurled his back. Over and over the assault continued. It was like watching the final death scene in a sci-fi movie.

"They fight hard for you," Abigail said. "They always have, and they will until the end."

"But what they don't know is that this isn't the end," Jan said. She motioned for me to continue watching the horrid attack.

Trent crawled to my side. Tears streaked down his face. He studied me for a while before straightening my legs and my arms. He wiped the blood from my mouth, and brushed the hair out of my face. He leaned over, stroked my face, and then kissed my lips.

"He doesn't even know he has the power," Abigail said.

He took my hand and held it to his chest, stroking my skin tenderly, completely unaware of the deadly exchange happening all around him. He didn't want to leave me. My eyes watered, my heart hurt, when I noticed a blue glow seep from his hand and wrap around his fingers — his aura. He had said it was blue. But how could I see it now? Was it because I was dead? Trent stared at his hands for a moment, at the light pouring out of him. He reached out to the cross around my neck. He touched it, almost timidly. When he did, sparks of light burst from the stone. A sparkly pink vapor poured out of it and covered my body. Trent watched, but didn't seem surprised at all.

"I put my energy source in the cross because I knew you would need it," Abigail said. "That's why I had to die. I also knew that if I gave this cross to Trent's grandfather, it would work its way to you. As the cross passed down through the Avila family, the energy stored inside it learned to respond to their touch, and I knew Trent would save you."

"One life for another," Jan said.

"Yes," Abigail agreed. "My life for yours, Dominique."

The image of Jan and Abigail started to fade. "No! You can't leave!" I reached out to them, grasping for their touch, but my hand passed right through their bodies.

"When you go back," Abigail said, "use the cross."

Jan added. "The cross is made of bloodstone, the stone of courage, the stone that has the power to overcome enemies, the stone that soldiers often carried into battle. You are a soldier."

"Wait! What do I do with the cross! How do I use it?" Their image continued blurring until they disappeared. The still and peaceful lake vanished, and I plunged into total darkness.

My eyes flew open. My chest tightened. I gasped for the heat-filled air.

Trent hovered over me. "Dominique! You're

alive!" Even though my ankles throbbed with pain, I got to my feet. He steadied me with his arms. "You, you, were dead," he said, his hands now cupping my face.

I hugged him tight. "You did it, Trent. You saved me." I noticed the others hadn't seen that I was alive. "And now I have to save the others."

Mom, Dad, and Farrell continued barraging Tavion with their blasts. Sparks flew through the air. The stench of sulfur, metal, and blood clogged my throat. I needed to get to Tavion, and fast. The daggers in my boots were gone, but then I thought of what Abigail had said about using the cross. I yanked it off my neck. It was pointed at the end—a cross that looked like a sword. But it wasn't a sword. It was more like a dagger!

"Dominique, what are you doing?"

A humming filled my ears, like the sound of an engine. I studied the cross, realizing the sound came from it, when it slowly expanded in my hands until it became a weapon— heavy and perfectly pointed. I held the tip to my palm, jabbed it into my skin, and raked it through. Blood dripped from the fresh wound and covered the weapon.

Trent grabbed my arm. "What the hell is going on?"

"I have to kill him, Trent. It's the only way. Please, you have to trust me."

He stared at me. I could tell he didn't want to release my arm. He looked at Farrell and my parents. They couldn't take much more. And he knew it. "Kill that asshole."

Head down, I ran through the blasts that flew by. I barreled into Tavion, knocking him to the ground, and rammed the cross-like dagger into his chest. I pushed down with all my strength, forcing the hilt deeper and deeper while my blood soaked through his open wound. Tavion howled and I screamed as his chest melted under my force. His eyes popped out of their sockets. Blood poured out all over the place. I shut my eyes tight and continued pressing the dagger into him until his shrieking stopped.

Strong steady hands gripped my shoulders. "Dominique," Farrell said. "You can let go now. It's over."

I forced my eyes open. Tavion had vanished. We were back on Galveston Island. Daylight had started streaking through the sky. A puddle of blood pooled all around me. The small black cross hung from its chain and draped over my bloodied hand. My hands trembled so violently it fell to the sand. Farrell picked it up and handed it to me. Mom and Dad fell to their knees, one on either side of me, and hugged me. Tears streamed down my face.

"What just happened?" Trent whispered.

I wiped my tears with the back of my hand and looked at my dad. "He can't know, can he?"

"No," Dad answered. "He can't."

Like back in my den after the first time Tavion attacked us, Trent's memory needed erasing. He couldn't remember anything he'd seen. It was better that way.

"Wait, I deserve an explanation," Trent said. "I need to know what the hell just happened."

I wanted to tell Trent everything, including the way I felt about him. Instead, I got up and put the cross in his hands. "Yes, you deserve to know everything. But you can't."

Shock and disbelief covered his face. I nodded at Farrell and Farrell went to Trent. He put his hand on Trent's shoulder. His white mist started to trickle out. Before Trent could object, Farrell's misty vapor swirled around Trent's feet and all over his body until Trent vanished.

Relief, sadness, and exhaustion swept through me. "Let's go home and get you cleaned up," Mom said.

My blood-soaked hands and clothes would be easy to clean. The hard thing would be moving on after everything I had been through because nothing would ever be the same.

CHAPTER
Twenty-five

I REMEMBERED LATE ONE NIGHT watching TV and flipping through the channels, stumbling upon the movie Psycho. It was the part where the guy stabbed a woman in the shower over and over, her blood mixing with the water and swirling around the bottom of the tub. Well, that was me. I was the woman. Tavion was the psycho guy. Unlike the victim in the movie, I had survived my attack. All that remained were my wounds and the mixture of Tavion's blood and mine that ran down my skin while I stood in the hot shower.

I had defeated the Tainted who had hunted me down and killed me in my eight prior lives. Even though I had finally beaten him, I didn't feel like the winner. I had lost too much in the process, had caused the death of too many people. More than that, I didn't even know who I was anymore.

My body shivered from the now cold water. I turned it off, stepped out, and wrapped myself in a towel. Even though it was soft and fluffy, I flinched with each touch, especially at my ankles that were cut and raw as was my right palm that I had gashed open. Farrell had offered to heal them, but I refused. The pain reminded me that everything I had been through was real. I needed that reminder. And then I wondered about my birthmark. I stood in front of the mirror, lifted my hair, and craned my neck. After everything that had happened, it was still there.

I grabbed a washcloth and started scrubbing. It had to come off, it just had to, but it didn't. A knock at the bathroom door stopped me from rubbing my skin raw.

"Dominique, it's Mom. Are you okay?"

I threw the rag in the sink. "I'm fine."

"Good. Can you please come downstairs when you're finished?"

Please come downstairs when you're finished means we need to talk, which was fine by me because I needed to know what would happen now that Tavion was dead. Did Mom and Dad expect me and Farrell to ease back into school as if nothing had happened? And what about Trent? Would he really not remember me dying and then coming back to life after he touched my cross? My cross! My hands shot to my neck. It was gone. And then I remembered putting it in Trent's hand before he vanished. He must still have it. At least, I hoped he did.

"Dominique, can you hear me? We need you to come downstairs."

"Sorry, I'll be there in a few minutes."

Drying my body, pulling my hair up in a ponytail, and getting dressed with all my cuts and bruises took longer than I thought. After about thirty minutes or so, I was downstairs. Mom, Dad, and Farrell sat at the kitchen table. Other than the crackling from the double-sided fireplace, the room was quiet. Too quiet. My body tensed. I took a seat on the stool by the kitchen island.

"Dominique," Dad said. "We're leaving Houston."

My mouth fell open. "What do you mean, leaving?"

Mom shifted in her chair. "Tavion may be dead, but in order to assure your safety, we've decided to leave Houston and go back to Michigan."

The crackling flames from the fireplace popped. A chill settled in my bones. "What do you mean, assure my safety?" Panic started budding inside me. "You're not saying that I'm still in danger, are you? I mean Tavion is dead, right?" My hand went to the back of my neck, at the mark that remained.

"Yes, he's dead," Farrell said. "We're only relocating to be on the safe side." He tilted his head and studied my face. "You did want to go back home to Michigan, didn't you?"

Yes, I definitely wanted to go back, but not like this. What would happen to Infiniti? I broke eye contact with Farrell. And what would happen to Trent?

"But we've already sold our house back there. Where will we go?" I asked.

"Your mother and I have been preparing for this day and have established a safe house up north on the Boardman River. In fact, that's where we were going when we were captured."

"The Boardman River, by Elk Rapids? Why not go back to Elk Rapids? Or even Traverse City?"

Dad walked to the armoire in the den. He came back with the picture of him and mom with their college friends. They stood in front of a cabin they went to every summer, arms linked and faces smiling. There were five people in the picture: Mom, Dad, a petite woman with freckles and short red hair, a tall guy with a long nose and stringy brown hair that tucked over his ears, and Ms. Ryken. Dad pointed at the people. "You know Colleen, and that's Richard and Sue. Richard and Sue own the cabin in the picture. It's right on the Boardman River."

"They're Pures, like us," Mom said. "They've been preparing for this day, too. They've shielded the entire area, and they're ready for us."

Richard and Sue looked happy, all of them did, even Colleen who belonged in a fashion magazine with her long, black hair and perfectly cut bangs. And of course, they all had true green eyes.

"So where's Colleen?" I asked.

"We're not sure," Dad said. "She disappears from time to time, working on other things."

Before I could ask what he meant by other things, Mom went on. "Dominique, when we leave, we'll tell everyone that we're taking you out of town to celebrate your birthday. We must cut all ties here. There can be no link to us."

"It will appear as if we crashed, and none of us survived," Dad said. "It's the only way to make sure we're safe. Including those we leave behind."

Crashed and died...like Veronica. My stomach clenched tight. How could I make Infiniti go through the death of another friend? How could I do that to her? I didn't even notice Mom's hand on mine until she spoke. "I'm so sorry, Dominique. But we have to do it this way. It's better for all involved. We leave in one hour."

Back in my room, I stared out the window, almost in a trance. It was barely eight in the morning. The sun had no chance of peeking through the thick gray clouds, and I thought it might even rain. I placed my injured palm against the window. The cold glass felt good against my cut. I dropped my hand and thought of the temperature back home. Here it was probably in the fifties, back home in the teens.

Like a robot, I started packing. If I concentrated on my actions, then I wouldn't have time to think about the consequences of faking our deaths and the impact it would have on the people who cared for us. And then my phone beeped. I wanted it to be Trent. Instead, it was a text from Infiniti.

U up? Wanna go 4 a walk around the lake?

This was it—my chance to say good-bye to my one true friend in Houston.

K. Meet u outside in 5.

I put on a jacket and went outside. Infiniti practically skipped down the sidewalk to meet me. Her wavy hair was pulled back in a high ponytail. She wore jean shorts and an A&M sweatshirt. "Guess what?" she asked in her sing-songy voice.

We walked across the street and to the lake. "What?"

"I got into A&M!"

The air smelled of rain, but there were no drops yet. I tried my best to put on a happy face. "That's great, Infiniti!"

With a spring in her step, she continued down the jogging trail. "You know, things are turning around, Dominique. I got into my number one school, my mom is being super cool right now, I've stopped smoking, and things with Billy are going great! This new year is gonna be my year! I can feel it!"

Hearing how happy she was made me feel better. Maybe leaving her behind wouldn't be so bad after all, and she'd be okay.

She stopped. "You know I could've never done this without you."

Guilt rippled through me. She had no idea the danger I had put her in. No idea the depth of sorrow still to come. "What do you mean?"

"I could've never gotten through the deaths of Veronica and Jan without you being there for me. You're my best friend, Dominique. Even though we haven't been friends that long, we've been through a lot. Life changing, true friendship stuff, ya know?"

A massive lump lodged in my throat. I cleared my throat. "Yeah, I know. I feel the same way."

Infiniti did most of the talking while we walked the mile path around the lake. I nodded here and there, but mostly bit the inside of my cheek as I forced myself not to lose it, guilt escalating with each step.

When we got back to my house, I told her I'd be leaving for a few days with my parents and

Farrell for San Antonio to celebrate my birthday. She gave me a big hug, told me to have fun, and then left.

I felt like shit.

The quiet house echoed my sadness as I went back to my room, sat on my bed, and stared at my ocean-colored walls. Droplets of water started hitting my window. Usually I liked the rain, but not today. It reminded me of the tears I held inside, tears I fought hard to bury away. My gaze landed on my snow globe. I picked it up and held it tight.

"Go to him," Farrell whispered.

He stood outside my door, and I wondered how long he'd been there.

"What?" I asked.

"Go. Say your good-byes." He buried his hands in his pockets.

Here he was, someone who had loved me for eight lifetimes, now nine, telling me to say good-bye to a guy he knew I cared about. My guilt magnified. Even though I couldn't figure out my feelings for Farrell this lifetime, it was clear that I once had strong emotions for him, but not as strong as the ones I had developed for Trent.

"Farrell, are you sure?"

"Yes."

I put the snow globe down. "Farrell, it doesn't mean—"

He raised his hand. "I know."

Before either one of us could change our minds, I left. The rain came down steady as I drove to Trent's. My palms were sweaty. My heart raced. When I got to his house, I was relieved to see his car in the driveway. I turned off the ignition to collect my thoughts for a minute. Farrell had erased his memory, but how far back did he go? I had no idea, but I had to see him.

I opened the car door and dashed to his house, my body shivering from the cold rain. I rang the doorbell before I lost my nerve. I heard footsteps approach the door, then stop. It was him, I knew it, and the fact that he had paused couldn't be a good sign. My heart sank. He opened the door with a stone-cold look on his face. I instantly regretted being there.

"Hi," I said, trying to sound normal. "Sorry to come by so early. I'm, uh, leaving out of town for a few days, so I thought I'd come by and see you, and say good-bye."

His silence made me uneasy. His eyes were distant. "Last time you were here you gave me my sweatshirt and told me we should stop hanging out. And now you're here to tell me that you're going out of town?"

So, that's the last thing he remembered. I felt like an idiot. "Well, yeah, I guess—"

"Here," he said. He handed me the bloodstone cross, the cross he had touched that had saved my life. "You must've dropped this when you were here, and for some crazy reason my grandmother still wants you to have it."

I was almost afraid to take it, but let him drop it into my hand anyway.

"Have a safe trip," he said, slamming the door in my face.

I walked back to my car through the rain, my heart aching while tears welled up in my eyes.

My vision blurred. I reached down to open my car door when a hand grabbed my arm. It was Trent, pulling me around to face him. We stood there, eyes locked, the rain coming down on us. He stared searchingly at me with his deep blue eyes that always made me weak at the knees.

"Why did you come here?" he asked.

"I… I… had to see you, Trent. I had to… see you… one last time."

He stepped close. He wrapped his hands around the back of my neck and pulled me to him. Our lips connected softly once, and then again and again and again. Each time our lips met, they lingered a little longer. Our bodies were wet with rain and desire as our kiss turned passionate and our bodies pressed hard against each other. Our tongues explored every inch of the other's mouth — over and over, neither one of us wanting to stop.

Finally, our kiss ended. His hands still wrapped around my neck and mine around his waist as we both tried to catch our breath. I pulled back and studied his beautiful face, sketching it forever in my memory.

"Good bye, Trent."

Before he could say anything, I turned, got in the car, and drove away without looking back.

When I got home, I went upstairs, changed clothes, and sat on my bed, ready to leave. I took one last look at my ocean-colored room. I thought of everything that had happened to me here in this city and the people who had made an impact on me — Infiniti, Veronica, Jan and Abigail. Lastly, I thought of Trent.

I took my snow globe and traced its cool glass with my fingertips. The town inside looked so peaceful, nothing like my life now. And even though I had wanted to go back home since moving, I didn't want it to be like this.

"You ready?" Farrell asked from the door. He saw the globe in my hands. Hurt flashed across his face before he looked away from me. I guess I couldn't blame him.

"I'm ready."

Before I put the globe back on my nightstand, I shook it. Snow covered the tiny town. Soon I'd be back in the snow, too. And even though it hurt to leave, I knew it was the right thing to do. I looked back at my room, my eyes lingering for a moment on everything I was leaving behind before I slowly shut the door.

FINAL STAND
Chapter One

COLD SEEPED INTO MY TIRED and achy bones as we drove away from our Houston home for the last time. Rain drizzled against the car windows. Thick, gray clouds filled the sky. The humming of the car lulled my mind until it became lost in the memory of the last two months.

My parents were Transhumans, or energy beings known as Pures, part of a race of humans that existed before mankind. Tavion, an evil Transhuman and leader of the Tainted, had marked me for death. He had even killed me in each of my past lives, but in this life, my final life, I had defeated him. And even though I had won, I didn't feel like the winner. Instead, I felt empty. Lost. Like I wasn't me anymore. Because I wasn't. Too much had happened. Too many had died—because of me.

"You okay?" Farrell whispered.

I studied his perfectly angular features and sympathetic green eyes before shifting away and staring out the backseat window. According to

Farrell, in each of my eight lives he'd fallen in love with me, and I had loved him back. But I didn't remember any of it. Even though flashes of memories of him would come to me now and again, and strong emotions for him had bubbled to the surface when we kissed, they didn't belong to me. Instead, they belonged to another version of me. Someone who didn't exist anymore.

"I'm fine," I muttered. I ran my fingertips over the rough bandages that covered my hand, my dry skin catching on the fabric. The only me that existed was the one who had sliced open her hand, covered her dagger with her blood, and plunged it into Tavion's chest and killed him; the one who had shared a passionate kiss with Trent Avila—a normal guy I'd never see again. I closed my eyes for a moment and pictured his face in my mind. Tan skin, brown hair with long bangs that hung into his deep blue eyes. His grandmother had given me the bloodstone cross that hung around my neck, and without it, I wouldn't have been able to defeat Tavion. Sadly, Trent would never know because Farrell had erased his memory.

Memory erased... That was it! A sliver of hope sprang in me. I'd ask Farrell to do that to me—wipe my mind. After all, he was my protector, and if erasing my life and starting over would help me, he'd have to do it. I snuck a glance his way. He rubbed his hands on his jeans and grabbed his knees. Emotional pain etched across his face. If only he didn't remember our past lives, our lost love, things would be easier for him. But he remembered everything, they all did. I was the only one who didn't. And that's when it hit me. He needed his memory erased, too. Like in the Men in Black movies. Flash a bright light in our eyes, insert a new memory, and live happily ever after.

If only…

With a heavy sigh, I wrapped myself in my soft blue blanket. Happily ever after didn't exist. But I did win. Tavion was dead. Yet here we were, leaving Texas and going back to Michigan and somewhere along the way faking our deaths in order to cut off ties with everyone we had ever known. I knew Mom and Dad wanted to be cautious, but taking off like this didn't seem like something a "safe" person would do. I couldn't help but wonder if they were keeping something from me.

The busy highway flanked by restaurants, bars, and car dealerships finally evolved into the open road. Cows and horses dotted the flat fields for miles and miles. Dad drove while Mom eyed the map, plotting our course home to Michigan.

"We'll cross Arkansas and go into Tennessee, stopping just outside Memphis. We'll stay there for the night." She folded the map on her lap and looked over her shoulder. "You may as well get some rest, Dominique. We've got a long day of driving ahead of us."

Rest? How could I? Doubts about my future turned my stomach upside down. Mixed emotions about Farrell and Trent plagued me. And then there was Infiniti — my one true friend who'd soon think I had died in a car crash. I wrapped my arms around my waist and told myself it was better for her to think I was dead. I just hoped she'd be okay.

Even though fatigue had settled deep in me, I had crossed over into that place where your brain can't shut down no matter how hard you try. And so my thoughts stretched out like an eternity while I watched the world creep past. Cows, fields, cows, fields, over and over. The peaceful solitude of the landscape entranced me. The repetitious thud of the windshield wipers swiping back and forth created the perfect background noise for slumber. After a while, my breathing deepened. My heart rate slowed. Finally, I drifted to sleep.

"Dominique, can you hear me?"

My body slept. Yet the voice calling out to me rang so clear in my head I could've sworn I was awake. A dream, it had to be a dream.

"Dominique, I'm here," the hoarse voice said again, this time urgent and prodding.

My heavy eyelids refused to open, as if weighted down by bricks and glued shut. Even the muscles in my body ignored my commands to move, get up, and find the voice calling me.

"You know who I am," the scratchy voice said again, louder this time.

My sleeping body tensed from a zap of fear. The voice belonged to Tavion. I'd recognize it anywhere. And it came from within me. An army of goose bumps dashed across my body. Wake up, I screamed to myself. Now!

"Waking won't help you, Marked One."

Panic rushed through me. My body jerked. My eyes flew open. Farrell sat close, his hands on my arm. "Hey, you alright?"

Mom studied me from over her shoulder. Dad peered at me through the rear-view mirror. I rubbed my eyes. "Yeah, I'm fine. I was just… having a bad dream."

"You sure?" Dad's eyes shifted from the road back to me. His brow creased with deep worry lines. He had spent his whole life worrying about me, hiding me from the Tainted, and protecting me from the truth that an evil Transhuman wanted me dead—the same evil Transhuman I had killed and who had just now invaded my dreams.

I cleared my throat. "I'm fine, Dad. Seriously. But I could use a bathroom break."

Mom kept a suspicious eye on me, not really believing my excuse. "We should be coming up on a rest stop in a few minutes. Can you wait?"

It was well past noon, and I had already held my bladder for a few hours. A few more minutes couldn't hurt. "Yeah, that's fine." I peeled off my blanket and combed my hair back with my stiff and achy hands when my stomach growled. "Guess I need some food, too."

Farrell kept his eyes on the road. I followed his line of sight out the window, at the fields we were passing. Was he worried about something? Did he know about my dream? I swallowed hard. Maybe I was still in danger and they weren't telling me.

"There we go," Mom said.

A gas station up ahead sprang into view. It sparkled white and blue with a flashing sign that promised clean bathrooms and juicy burgers. Peering at the neon signs, I realized the cloud and rain from the morning had disappeared. I placed my fingertips on the window. Still cold, even though the sun shone bright. Dad parked in front of a grassy area with picnic tables. He thrummed his fingers against the steering wheel before turning off the ignition, then turned and looked at Farrell. "Stay close to Dominique."

My body tensed. "What? Why does—"

"Dominique," Mom placed her hand on Dad's knee, as if to silence him. "Some habits are hard to break."

Her words were meant to make me feel better, but fell far short. A nervous laugh escaped my lips. "If I were in danger, you guys would tell me, right? I mean, Tavion is dead. We did win." Another laugh rushed out of me. "Right?"

Farrell reached out to me. "Yes. Tavion is dead."

Dead yet violating my dreams, I thought to myself, not wanting to tell them I had just heard his voice. It would only worry them more than they already were. They didn't need that. Plus, I didn't want them hovering over me.

Dad rubbed his stubbled face and sighed. "I'm sorry, Dominique. Your mom is right. Old habits." He opened his car door. "Come on, stretching our legs and getting a bite will do us good."

The cool crisp air filled my lungs, replacing the stuffy air from the car. Even the grassy, earthy scents from the nearby fields smelled good. As we got closer to the entrance of the gas station, we passed a silver car parked at the gas pump. A golden retriever stretched his head out the back window, nose sniffing the air, tongue hanging out. When he spotted us, his eyes locked on me.

His ears lay back. He bared his teeth and growled. I froze, afraid he'd jump out the window and attack.

"Rexie, down!" a woman called out from inside the car.

Farrell stepped between me and the dog and wrapped his arm around my waist. He pointed at the dog. "It's okay, boy." A spark flickered from his fingertip, right at the dog. The retriever let out a whine and sat back.

The woman praised the dog for calming down while I started to panic. Dogs usually loved me. Farrell swiftly ushered me inside.

"What happened?" Mom asked, peering over my shoulder at the car we had just passed.

"That dog freaked when he saw me." I didn't realize how fast my heart was beating until Farrell squeezed my hand. A warm peaceful feeling rushed over me like it always did when he touched me—followed by a deep yearning for him.

"Some canines are like that," Farrell explained. "He probably sensed your recent conflict with Tavion." Another squeeze calmed me even more. "I wouldn't worry about it, Dominique."

My breathing steadied. My heart rate slowed. Butterflies fluttered in my stomach. Farrell held onto my fingertips for a second before letting my hand fall. I almost reached back out for him, but didn't. "Thanks, Farrell."

Mom's worried face relaxed. "Come on, let's go to the restroom." She walked to the back of the gas station as if everything was okay. As if I was just her daughter and she was just my mother. As if I hadn't killed an evil energy being the night before.

My thoughts filled with memories of Tavion as I went to the restroom and washed my hands. As I lathered the soap, mom joined me. I looked up at the mirror, catching our reflection. I was almost her exact replica. Long brown hair, tall and slender. Her eyes sparkled true green while mine were dark olive, sometimes gray. My gaze lingered on hers. True green eyes—the mark of a Pure.

"Why are my eyes different?" I shook the water off my hands and grabbed a paper towel. "I mean, they should be like yours and Dad's and Farrell's, right?"

She tugged out some paper towel, too. "Yes, as a descendant of Pures you should have eyes like ours, but you don't. You never have." She tossed the paper in the trash.

"I've never had eyes like you and Dad? Not in any of my…" I whispered, even though I knew we were alone, "past lives?"

"No," Mom answered. She turned me to her and held my face. "You've always had beautiful olive-colored eyes."

Tavion's thin, pale, wrinkled face popped into my mind. His eyes were dark as night. I thought of Fleet, Farrell's brother, originally a Pure who had turned and joined Tavion's ranks and who had been killed during our final confrontation. What color were his eyes? I couldn't remember. "And the Tainted have black eyes?"

"Yes, they do. But sweetheart, it doesn't matter." She stroked my hair and tucked a strand behind my ear. "All that matters is this is over. We made it. And we're all okay."

Something inside me said not to believe her, but I ignored it. I needed something to hold onto. "I hope you're right."

"Of course, I am." She smiled. "Now let's get some food."

We met up with Dad and Farrell at the burger counter and placed our order. While we waited, people rushed in and out of the station, and each time, Dad and Farrell went on alert. Dad caught my worried glance right away. "Sorry, Dominique. Remember — old habits."

Yeah, right, I thought. My gaze wandered over to the girl getting our food together. She looked to be around seventeen, like me. She wore tons of make-up and smacked her gum like she didn't have a care in the world. How lucky to have a simple life.

"Here's your order," she said. Farrell took the bags and thanked her, causing a sigh to escape her lips while her cheeks turned red. Farrell smiled and when he did a sharp pang of jealousy jabbed inside me. I turned away from him, embarrassed and confused about my feelings. I mean, could I really blame her for having that reaction around Farrell? He was gorgeous. And that's when I realized I had feelings for him — true emotions of my own and not connected to anything that might've been between us. So why was I resisting him?

He positioned himself in front of me and tilted his head. "You feeling okay?"

I grabbed one of the bags, suddenly feeling exposed and vulnerable. "Yep," I huffed, with a hint of irritation in my voice.

Before he could say anything else, I led the way out of the station and to the picnic tables. The cars that had stopped for gas or food had traveled on. It was just us. Alone. Surrounded by a cool breeze and bright sun. And yet, the weight of everything we had been through back in Houston kept me cold and dark inside. I wondered if they felt it, too.

We laid out our things and ate in silence. I thought of their plan to fake our deaths. How would we pull something like that off? The cheeseburger I nibbled at tasted worse with each bite. The stale bun and bland meat turned my stomach. I washed it down with a gulp of flat lemonade and pushed my food aside. "So, how exactly are we going to fake our deaths?"

Dad wiped his mouth. "The plan is for Colleen to meet up with us tomorrow morning. We'll ignite our car in such a way that it'll look like a mechanical explosion. The fire will be so intense there will be no human remains."

Shivers cascaded up and down my body. Farrell sat closer, his leg touching mine. I almost inched away, but decided I wanted him near, and not just for his calming effect. "And everyone will think it's us?" My gaze met Mom's and Dad's before resting on Farrell. "Is that really going to work?"

Silence hung in the air. I pictured Infiniti and Trent learning about the crash. I knew Infiniti would be devastated. Trent, too. I threw my half-eaten food in the nearby trashcan. "Have we tried this in any other life?"

Farrell angled his body to me. "No, but I'm

pretty confident it'll work. If everything goes as planned."

Any ounce of hope I had quickly vanished. "Whoa, wait a second. If everything goes as planned? That doesn't sound very reassuring."

Dad cleared off the rest of the table. "Well, right now we have no idea where Colleen is."

Colleen—a Pure who had disguised herself as my teacher. She had a wise air about her, an authority that surpassed that of my mom and dad. Even Farrell. "So what's up with her? What's her story? And where is she?"

"She's the oldest of the Pure and has a lot of power," Dad said. "And unfortunately, we haven't been able to contact her all day." He rubbed his temples. "If she's missing, or something has happened to her, it can only mean something bad."

I shivered. "Something worse than Tavion?"

"For lifetimes we've never survived past your confrontation with Tavion," Farrell explained. "So whatever happens from here on out is completely new." He touched my fingers. "But nothing can be worse than what we've already been through, okay?"

"We're just all flying blind," Mom said. "And we're not used to it."

"Join the club," I muttered.

Nobody spoke as we drove the rest of the day and into the night. We were all on equal footing now, and no one knew what our future would hold. But I had to believe Farrell when he said that whatever might happen next couldn't be bad. After all, what could be worse than being hunted and killed for lifetimes?

About the Author

ROSE GARCIA IS A LAWYER turned writer who's always been fascinated by science fiction and fantasy. From a very young age, she often had her nose buried in books about other-worlds, fantastical creatures, and life and death situations. More recently she's been intrigued by a blend of science fiction and reality, and the idea that some supernatural events are, indeed, very real. Rose's books feature gut-wrenching emotional turmoil and heart-stopping action. Rose is known for bringing richly diverse characters to life as she draws on her own cultural experiences. Rose lives in Houston with her husband and two kids. You can visit Rose at:

WWW.ROSEGARCIABOOKS.COM.

55185673R00167

Made in the USA
Columbia, SC
13 April 2019